Champagne Kisses

KATHERINE E. WEBB

Contents

For my mother, who I hope would have loved this book, and everything her daughter has become. Your voice and laughter will remain in my head forever.

Author's Note

This book contains depictions of fatphobia & body-shaming, disordered weight & body thoughts, racism, bullying, and therapy to overcome childhood trauma. Cheating, the death of a grandparent, and queermisia are also addressed. If these topics are triggering for you, please proceed with care. I attempted to handle these sensitive topics as thoughtfully as possible.

Prologue

MAYA

September 1997

```
Ms. Nappy Head
```

<u>**Thunder thighs!**</u>

TRY JENNY CRAIG!!!

Call me when you lose 50 pounds, LOL

I clap the worn composition book closed and lean back against the painted concrete bricks of the stall behind me. The putrid yellow of the walls is fitting, considering I might actually be sick. I *knew* I should have started my own book! No one talks shit about you when it's *your* slam book.

I crack the book open again to see crude depictions of myself in pen and Sharpie. I could've done without the drawings. Do they think I don't know about my thunder thighs? God, I hope Tim and James haven't seen this.

Before I can continue to spiral, Tiffany pops her head over the top of the bathroom stall in which I've sequestered myself. No one needed to see me have a full-on meltdown in the middle of the choir room. That would've been the cherry on top of this shit sundae of a day.

"Maya, are you crying in there?" I quickly wipe my tears with my sleeve, keeping my head down so she can't see.

"Uh, no. Of course not!" Tiffany looks at me doubtfully, so I push the corners of my mouth up into what I hope passes for a smile. Tiffany despises pity parties.

"I'm fine. Really. Just stressed about the history test next period." Tiffany raises her eyebrow to let me know she's not buying my bullshit excuse, but hops off the neighboring commode when I stand. Unfortunately, I can't stay in here forever;

the smell of disinfectant is making me dizzy. I suppose it's better than any alternative for a junior high bathroom.

I flush my tissues and step out of the stall, but the slam book slips from under my arm onto the bathroom floor. Tiffany kicks it out of my reach and snatches it up victoriously.

"Ah ha! I *knew* you were in there with Julie's slam book." She holds it away from her with just her fingertips like it's radioactive. "Why do you bother reading it? You know she's got it in for you and she's just going to pass it around to all the cheer bitches." She flips through the book and rolls her eyes dramatically when she gets to my page.

I appreciate the show of support, but as one of our school's resident bombshells, Tiffany can't possibly understand what I'm going through. Seriously, she's got, like, the perfect body, long black hair, and hazel eyes. Tiffany's barely five feet, but she's got the presence of a freight train and a temper to match. People practically clear a path whenever they see her coming. Meanwhile, I'm stuck with boring brown eyes and, as the slam book so eloquently put it, a "nappy head" and fifty extra pounds, mostly in my thighs. My cool points go up just from standing next to her.

She lets out an unladylike snort when she's done reading.

"'Maya the Pariah', huh? Bet it took someone *all five* of their brain cells to come up with that one." She snaps the book shut without bothering to check her page. How does she do that? Then again, her page is probably just compliments anyway.

"I know, I know. I'm a glutton for punishment. I was just curious." I tuck the book back into my backpack and nibble on my fingernails.

"Do you think Tim has seen it?" Tiffany levels me with a "you've got to be kidding me" face and I wish I could take the question back.

"Considering he's Julie's boyfriend? Yeah, I think he's seen it. I think he was the first person to write in it right before he fingered her while watching 'I Know What You Did Last Summer' for the fiftieth time." She turns and wraps her arms around herself to look like two people making out and I giggle behind my hands.

"Ew, gross, Tiffany! How do you come up with this stuff?" Tiffany just smirks and shrugs.

"It's a gift. You should really try it; let those cheer bitches know Maya's not some goody two-shoes."

I sigh and lean against the wall.

"But I *am* a goody two-shoes. All those anonymous questions in Sex Ed last year totally blew my mind."

Tiffany leans against the wall next to me and sighs like she's remembering a fond memory.

"Ah, yes. Who can forget Danny Raskin asking about the purpose of areolas? And then Mr. Drummond saying they're bullseyes?! I almost peed myself laughing."

The bathroom echoes with our laughter; that *was* the funniest Biology class ever.

"How'd you know it was Danny? Those questions were anonymous."

Tiffany just scoffs.

"It was hardly anonymous when he bragged about it all through lunch."

When it came to Sex Ed, the boys had been especially shameless. I shake my head realizing I'm no longer worried about the slam book. She might not really get what I'm going through, but she's always been able to pull me out of my funk.

Tiffany pushes off the wall abruptly.

"New topic: What are you going to wear to the homecoming dance? Once again, I'm stuck with whatever I can find at Goodwill." She sighs dramatically. She might have the perfect body, but her family doesn't have much money for new clothes.

That's my cue. I reach into my backpack and pull out a clear garment bag containing a tea-length, burgundy dress with spaghetti straps and a floral shawl. Despite the fluorescent lighting, the dress still shimmers.

"Actually, I made something for you to wear. I snagged some premium satin in about six different colors and figured I'd try out one of my new patterns for a homecoming dress." Tiffany grabs the dress from me before smoothing her hands over the garment bag reverently.

"I made one for myself too. It's in a different color, though, so we won't be too matchy-matchy." She blinks rapidly to push back the tears forming in her eyes. I seriously hope those are tears of joy; the last person who made fun of her thrift store clothes wound up with a bloody nose.

"This is amazing, Maya! Thank you so much." She holds the garment bag against herself and spins. "I am going to look *fierce* in this." She hugs me with one arm, keeping the dress safe in the other.

"More importantly, we're going to break some hearts this weekend. No one will remember that stupid slam book come Monday." She grabs me by the hand and pulls me toward the door. "Now come on. Let's get to class."

Mom and Dad drop me off in front of the building just as the dance is scheduled to start. I smooth my sweaty palms over my dress. It's a lot like the one I made for Tiffany except it's royal blue and off the shoulder to hide my upper arms. *Did the slam book have it right? Am I too big? What if no one wants to dance with me? Ugh, maybe I should just hide in the choir room until it's all over.*

Tiffany hops out of an old Ford truck, pairing the dress I made her with the floral Doc Martens she got firsthand as a birthday present a month ago. Once again, her arrival saves me from spinning out and I run to see the dress close up.

"You look amazing, Tiff! I never would have thought to wear it with the Doc Martens but you look cool, like 'Clarissa

Explains it All'." Tiffany preens under my compliments and I notice she has on eye shadow, mascara, and red lipstick while all my parents let me wear is lip gloss. Yet another reason she will always be cooler than me.

The cafeteria has been transformed from the linoleum-lined gauntlet of my recurring nightmares, into an enchanted forest. Cardboard trees dot the dance floor, construction paper flowers and exotic animals line the walls, and crepe paper in various shades of green and brown hangs from the ceiling like vines. There are even colorful party lights like the ones at laser tag. It's magical.

As usual, we're some of the first people in the cafeteria. Despite my minor panic attack earlier, our clique tries never to miss even one minute of a school dance. We might not be the best dancers, but the music rocks and the dark offers cover for those of us too shy to talk to the opposite sex during the day. Plus, missing a dance means missing out on some of the juiciest gossip. Who can forget when half the girls' volleyball team got suspended for drinking Everclear in the teachers' lounge?

The DJ plays Red Hot Chili Peppers, Spice Girls, and Usher as the room steadily fills up with kids. During the slow songs, I crack my friends up with interpretive dances instead of waiting for a guy to approach me.

Out of the corner of my eye, I see James come in. He's hanging with Tim, Julie, and a few other kids from yearbook. *All* the popular kids take yearbook.

Tim is cute but Tiffany is right; he's with Julie. I value my life too much to crush on him for real. James, however, is single and looks just like Shawn from "Boy Meets World". His eyes are deep royal blue instead of the usual sky blue, freckles dust his nose and cheeks, and his chestnut brown hair falls in waves, partially obscuring his eyes. Whenever I'm near him, my whole body starts to sweat and I can't stop blushing. I feel the same as when I stay up late to see the sexy movies on Cinemax—"Skin-emax", as Tiffany calls it. Tiffany sees me see him and dances over to whisper in my ear.

"Go for it, girl! What's the worst that could happen?" I look over at him and another wave of desire makes me want to actually fan myself.

"Oh, I don't know. Public rejection? Complete humiliation?" There is no *way* I'm going over there. Tiffany just laughs and rolls her eyes.

Our dance circle has grown, with more friends from choir, almost the whole brass section from band, and even a few jocks from the basketball team. Everyone is dancing together, regardless of their clique; another bonus of school dances.

A few songs later and I feel a little sweatier and a whole lot braver. James and his group are dancing near us and he hasn't left to make out with a girl like he did last time...n-not that I was watching! I use a paper towel I snuck into my bra on the last bathroom run to blot my face and sneak yet another peek at James. Why *can't* I ask him to dance? It's not like I'm asking him to be my boyfriend.

Monica's "For You I Will" comes on like a sign from God and I seize the moment before I can chicken out. James turns towards me right as I'm about to tap his shoulder.

"Um...Hey, James. Uh...Do you m-maybe...wanna dance?" I can barely make eye contact but, to my surprise, he actually smiles at me.

"Hey, Maya. I'd—"

"Is this person *bothering* you, James?" I turn to see Julie and her boyfriend sneering like bullies in an 80s movie. Shit! Why is she torturing me? Did I do something to her in a past life? James' smile is gone and with it, all hope of avoiding complete humiliation.

"Shouldn't you be back at the farm with the other pigs, Maya?" She snorts for the full effect, her voice dripping with malice. She's clearly enjoying this.

I wish I could melt into the floor. From the embarrassed look on his face, James feels the same way. I guess that means he's not going to stick up for me.

Tiffany notices the impending train wreck and shoves in between us to defend my honor, but I don't stay to watch. I run down the hall and hide in the choir room, just like I should've done from the beginning. Whatever I did to Julie in a past life must have been unforgivable. My face is wet with tears and my chest actually aches. Tiffany was right about at least one heart getting broken this weekend: mine.

CHAPTER ONE

Adam

Present Day

There they are! I pull my earbuds from the pocket of yesterday's jeans and switch my phone to bluetooth. It had gotten so hot, I worried I might get first degree burns. Emily keeps going, either oblivious to or intentionally ignoring the noise coming from my end of the line during my search. As I listen to her yammer on about woodwind quintets and peonies, I consider just leaving my phone in the living room and going on about my evening. I doubt she'd even notice. Why the hell did Bryan make me his best man?

We met freshman year as roommates at Stanford. He got to campus four days after I did and actually had professional movers. With his half of the room brought to you by Restoration Hardware and mine straight from the IKEA catalog, we were opposites from the beginning.

Though he looked like your standard All American Abercrombie & Fitch model, complete with blonde hair, blue eyes, and a tan from surfing some beach in San Diego, his family was actually Italian and from the Upper East Side in New York. His dad's even an Italian chef. His mom is essentially a socialite; she may have released her own line of jewelry at one point.

Bryan was a legacy, and studied about as hard as you can expect from someone whose family's name was on the West wing of the Humanities Center. He graduated with a Bachelors in Psych and a solid C average. I, on the other hand, stayed up most nights cramming for a final or practicing my coding, and I graduated with a 3.9 in Computer Science.

He did every extracurricular available: the Stanford Italian Society, the Stanford Alpine Club, the Nature Photography Club, the Stanford Wine Society, and the Stanford Democrats. I joined the Korean-American Student Society, but I probably only came to five meetings my whole time there. I did get pretty involved with the Stanford Video Game Association, but what self-respecting Computer Science major within ten miles of Silicon Valley wouldn't?

Sure, I roomed with him all four years of college, and yes, we both chose New York over the West Coast after graduation (Bushwick for me and back to the Upper East Side with his parents for Bryan), but that hardly makes me qualified to counsel anyone on true love, vows, and the many, *many* compromises of marriage. I've never had a girlfriend serious enough for a three-day weekend, let alone three month's salary for a diamond ring.

Hell, keeping things casual (very casual!) with the ladies is one of the few things Bryan and I have in common. *Used to*, anyway. Neither of us had the time or the inclination for anything serious, until he met Jessi. Then suddenly he's blowing off drinks, bringing her to meet his family, and grabbing brunch. Fucking *brunch*! No self-respecting bachelor has ever grabbed brunch with a woman he was sleeping with; it sends all the wrong signals. Signals like "I love you," "I see a future with you," and "Let's get married."

At least Emily's around to take the lead with all this wedding bullshit. As Bryan's younger sister, the Maid of Honor, and one of the most sought after event planners in New York City, she was the obvious choice. She's Type A to a "T", like the main chick from "Legally Blonde" minus the chihuahua. I'm just the token penis so she can say she consulted a guy during the planning. It's unlikely she'll give me anything major to do out of fear I'll fuck it up. Maybe I'll luck out and just get to plan the bachelor party.

But there's one small hiccup in what would otherwise be a cushy setup: she's half in love with me. I've never told Bryan, even after she showed up drunk in nothing but a trench coat the night before graduation. That was awkward. When I declined her offer to role-play "Bugsy" with me as her "private dick", she took it like a champ but has been sure to let me know the offer is still on the table all these years later. Fingers crossed she'll rein it in for the sake of being in the wedding party. In my experience, though, weddings make women *more* horny, not less. Yeah, being Bryan's best man is gonna be a blast.

I hide my annoyed sigh with a weak cough and try to buck myself up. There's always a chance I'll get to hook up with one of the bridesmaids. Bryan's fiancee, Jessi, is a Broadway actress. Chorus girls flexible enough to be Rockettes plus Emily's sorority sisters means a wealth of options at all the wedding events. Maybe Bryan was actually doing me a solid.

Emily still hasn't noticed I've been tuning her out through her last few bullet points.

"...already booked the venue, because the property manager told me someone called RIGHT after me for the same date and time. Can you believe that?"

"No shit? That's crazy," I said, summoning all my powers not to just hang up.

"Wow. Is the wedding of your best friend and college roommate really *that* boring?," she asks, her voice filled with humor. I guess she *had* noticed I wasn't listening. I chuckle in return.

"Sorry, Em. I'm just no good with this stuff. Give me batch files and schema and I'm golden, but photo booths and..." I try to remember some of the terms she'd mentioned. "...Uh, topiaries? That's hardly my style. If it were me, I'd just go to the Justice of the Peace."

If we weren't on the phone, I know Emily would be rolling her eyes at me.

"Well, thank goodness everyone doesn't feel like you do, otherwise I'd be out of a job."

"True that. Cheers to late-stage capitalism!"

"Don't you talk about Sombart to me, pal. You're not the only one on this call with a degree from Stanford. Plus, last time I checked, working for a Fortune 500 telecom company isn't exactly sticking it to 'the man'." Though she kept her tone playful, I can tell I wouldn't want to be on her bad side. Event planning was definitely Emily using her powers for good and not evil.

"Truce, OK? I was only teasing." Ever the professional, she changes the subject.

"I hope you boys keep it classy during the bachelor party. It's the weekend before the wedding and there won't be enough time to clean up any serious..." I hear her pause, searching for the word. "...messes." I laugh out loud.

"What kind of messes?"

"I don't know. A tattoo, shaved head, broken leg; use your imagination," she replies.

"Sure thing, boss. I'm as classy as they come."

"I mean it, Adam," she says with warning in her voice. "Don't you dare do anything to mess up my wedding."

"*Your* wedding?" No *way* am I letting that slip by.

"You know what I mean." I can tell she's trying to hide her embarrassment, so I let it drop. It doesn't take Sherlock Holmes to see she's the marrying type. Probably been planning her wedding since she was six. I use my own project management powers and get this conversation back on track.

"So, what are my action items? Do I need to set up keg delivery? Vet the strippers? They have strippers at engagement parties, right?"

Emily giggles lightly.

"Ha ha," she says dryly. "I *knew* you weren't listening! I chose this venue because they're practically full-service. I used them for the Garcia wedding a couple month's back, and they were flawless. Of course, Dad is bringing his sous chef, saucier, and pastry chef to handle catering. Also, me and the other brides-maids are coming early to do a surprise engagement gift for Jessi. All that's left is to review and revise the guest list, approve the proofs for all the stationary, and bring the party favors. And since I figured you wouldn't want to deal with the guest list and proofs…?"

She drops the rest of the sentence for me to fill in the blank. She's totally right. I'd probably break out in hives if I had to spend even a second debating fonts or different shades of white. Plus, the guest list is likely to be a tedious nightmare; I'll bet Emily lives for that kind of thing.

"Got it. I'll handle the favors. Do you think Etsy sells classy beer Koozies?" While I laugh, I can almost hear Emily's brow furrowing over the phone.

"Hmmm. Maybe I should handle favors, too," she says, clear-ly not appreciating my humor. Yet another reason I dodged a bullet with her that night all those years ago.

"Emily, c'mon. I'm kidding. I may not be from the Upper East Side, but I can pick out scented candles or custom boxes of chocolate like nobody's business," I offer.

"Just shoot me a text for approval before you hit 'buy'," she hedges.

"Deal," I agree. I knew NYC's biggest control freak wouldn't leave me to my own devices. I hear her relieved sigh and then...

"I'm glad I can count on you, Adam. You know...I'd be happy to come over and help you go through a few options. You could even help me drink this great bottle of Bordeaux I got from a client. I think one bottle a week is the most you're allowed to drink alone before you need to seek help," she laughs.

There it is. She is offering, again, to come over to my place for a nightcap. I get it: I've known her brother and, by association, her, for quite some time. But you don't shit where you eat. That's one of those core male values of the universe, along with "bros before hos".

"I think I can handle the favors, but thanks, Em. Listen, I have an early meeting," *and I'm tired of having this conversation*, I finish in my head. "I promise I'll text before I buy and be sure to send you the receipt once they're purchased. Can we connect again sometime next week?" *Or maybe next month?* No reason for us to spend any more time together than necessary.

"Okay, sounds good," she says quietly. I pretend not to notice the disappointment in her voice and hang up.

Outside the windows of my apartment, it looks to be after seven o'clock. Hopefully all our calls aren't that long. The sun is low in the sky, peeking between the apartment buildings and the elevated J train. The street lights are starting to come on and the ice cream trucks head back to wherever it is they go when they're not dealing out sugary sweets to kids across the five boroughs. As always, Bachata is playing full blast from an old stereo in the bodega on the corner. Brooklyn in the Summer really comes alive.

After a crazy day at work, plus that endless call, I definitely need to wash off the day. I kick off my Converse All Stars and leave a trail of dark jeans, one of my prized vintage tees, and a flannel on my way to the shower. Thank goodness CloudTech is casual because I could *not* do a tie for forty hours a week.

I step out of my boxers, turn on the rain shower head, and adjust the temperature to just short of scalding. Standing under the spray, I let out a groan as the hot water erases all thoughts of weddings, server issues, and budget meetings. All of that can wait until later. I squeeze a dollop of coconut shea butter body wash into my loofah and scrub my arms, my chest, my stomach. I swipe further down and run into my perpetual wingman. Lately, he's been standing at attention almost constantly.

My dick juts out from the suds at the base of my abs—thick and lightly veined. The weight of my balls in my hands as I lather them reminds me that it's been longer than usual since my last lady visitor. She was saved in my phone as "Legs4Days", and, though I made my intentions clear from jump, she tried to spend the night, pretending to be asleep when I nudged her away after the customary fifteen minutes of snuggling. It sucks when they can't (or won't) take the hint.

"I had a great time, but I have an early game with my buds tomorrow," I'd said, which was true. Sex and flag football are essential for my sanity. After a little pouting, she dropped it and called an Uber. She knew we weren't a love connection. We were just two people using a warm body to blow off a little steam.

Later, things turned hectic at work, and I've been head down in team building sessions and change requests ever since. Some days it's even hard to find time to jerk off. My coworkers tend to avoid me on those days.

It's for the best; it's been getting harder and harder to find women interested in sex with no strings attached. A woman who's fine without the boyfriend bullshit is practically a unicorn these days. I blame Beyonce. Not all women deserve the ring. First it's snuggling, then it's brunch, then you're meeting the parents and trying to spend every waking moment with her like some simp.

Bryan's my boy and I'm happy for him—I'm not going to be some asshole best man trying to talk him out of marrying Jessi. *What a cliché.* Jessi's not only awesome, but her dancer friends would probably high kick me right in the nuts if I did anything to screw up her wedding. Even so, I honestly don't get the appeal. As long as no one's getting hurt, why bother with the complicated shit like *expectations* and *commitment?*

My mom would probably drag me to church if she knew I felt like this.

"What about your father and I, Adam?" she would day. *"Don't you want what we have with someone special?"*

And she would have a point. Mom and Dad have been married thirty years. They raised five kids from hyperactive knuckleheads to successful adults. They own their home outright, and still saved enough that none of us had to take out more than ten grand in school loans.

But all of that isn't for everyone, and I know firsthand that it's *hard fucking work.* For some people, a physical connection between two consenting adults with an itch to scratch and a meeting in the morning is enough. We fuck, and then we head home for a good night's sleep in our own beds.

Now in the shower, leaning against the granite walls while the steam builds, I grab the base of my dick and try to imagine my perfect woman. What *would* it take for me to settle down?

She'd have to be beautiful. I love a woman with big, soulful eyes that make my mouth dry. And she'd have to have great T&A. My bros insist you're either a tits man, or an ass man, but I'm proof you can be both. My shaft throbs painfully as I think about my perfect woman's curves, her smooth skin.

She'd be eager to please, dropping down on her knees and unzipping me as soon as I got through the door. I'm a bit of a freak, and I'd need someone who can hang. Her warm mouth would swallow the head of my dick and circle it with her tongue. She'd let me cum in her mouth and then I'd fuck her missionary style in my bed.

People don't give missionary enough props, I think as I stroke faster, drops of precum immediately washed away by the spray of the shower. It's got so many variations—traditional, off the side of the bed, with her ankles up by her ears—and it's the perfect angle to rub on a woman's clit and make her start speaking in tongues before her pussy tries to choke your dick to death. Sex might not come with flowers, but for my partners, it always comes with an orgasm.

I think about my perfect woman's round hips and start to tighten my grip, increasing the friction. We'd do doggy next, those full, soft hips the perfect handlebars to get a really deep stroke. I'd make her ass jiggle every time I pushed all the way home.

"Ahh, fuck!" I shout, shooting thick ropes of cum against the shower wall. I lean back against the tiles, a little out of breath. Even just the *thought* of my perfect woman is dangerous. Luckily, keeping it casual nearly eliminates the risk of ever finding her.

I angle the shower head to rinse off the wall and suds up my now empty balls. That should hold me until maybe...tomorrow? I groan to myself, still worked up. Sometimes my high sex drive is a curse. A visit to someone on my roster or maybe a new lady friend might be in order.

I finish washing up and step out of the shower, still feeling a bit edgy. I can't solve my sexual frustration tonight, but I can order those party favors.

CHAPTER TWO

Maya

I drop my purse and keys on the entryway table and immediately notice my site's webpage is still open. Huh. That's weird. Why didn't it go to sleep while I was out?

I move closer and see a blinking popup with an error message; it looks like there was a glitch with the scheduler. Damnit! I thought for sure I turned on the service delay message! Rico, my usual engraver, is on vacation for the next two weeks, and the message was *supposed* to let customers know engraving services will take extra time.

With Rico away, I have to use my backup engraver, Jerry. Don't get me wrong; Jerry does good work, but he handles engraving for a ton of clients, so he takes about twice as long. When you run an online shop selling personalized *everything* (from shirts, to mugs, to key chains), fast turnaround is key if you want to move enough volume to break even.

I bite my nails nervously. I think it's time to invest in my own engraving tool, at least for the small jobs. I'll need to run the ROI for that, considering I might not even have the *time* to do my own engraving with all my other orders. And I just got my embroidery machine for big jobs two months ago? Hmm... Maybe I should stop engraving all together and focus exclusively on sewing, needlepoint, and embroidery. Ugh, but then Rico is out of a job! I'd hate to have to let him go after finally being able to hire another person.

I manually turn on the service delay message—double-checking the green, "Active" flag is on this time—and open up the one order that came through.

Customer Name: Adam Park

Item: Champagne toasting flute; 14K gold trim

Quantity: 175

Personalized?: Yes

Message:

Bryan & Jessi

Cheers to forever!

Delivery Date: June 28, 2024

Last Four Digits of Credit Card: 9275

Shit, shit shit!! That's less than two weeks away! Why couldn't Rico just skip taking a vacation for multiple years in a row like a normal American? Then again, what sane person would pass up seeing Machu Picchu in person? Rico could've handled such a tight timeline no problem, but I've got my doubts about Jerry.

Bracing myself for the worst, I push away from my makeshift office (it's really just a board on top of four bins of thread, yarn, and assorted beads in the corner of my living room) and begin to pace my tiny kitchen while dialing Jerry. I rarely stand still when I'm on the phone. Something about the movement takes the sting off bad news, or gets me even more hyped about good news. But not even the pacing, my sunny, yellow walls, or the peach galette I have cooling on the counter are enough to brighten my spirits at the thought of not being able to deliver this order. Jerry's brittle voice picks up after just one ring.

"Hellooooo, Ms Maya." Jerry has a sing-song greeting and insists on calling me "Ms Maya". He also insists I call him Jerry instead of Mr. Rossi, even though it goes against all of my home training. *Please, call me Jerry. Mr. Rossi's my father,* "he'd said when I first called him after finding his listing in the industry directory. Old people always think that's the funniest joke.

"Hello, Jerry?" I start nervously. "I hope it's not too late to call." 8:30pm certainly isn't too late for me, but Jerry's seventy-five years old and a bit old-fashioned to boot.

"Of course not, Ms. Maya. How old do you think I am?" Could Jerry read minds? I know I hadn't said that aloud. I clear my throat awkwardly.

"Oh, Jerry. I was just trying to be respectful of my elder, even though I wouldn't guess you were a day over forty," I lied. Jerry definitely looked a day over forty—11,000 of them. He laughed good-naturedly anyway.

"What do you need, dear?"

"I just got an order for 175 engraved champagne flutes…They need them in two weeks for an event on Cape Cod. I was hoping–"

"Sorry, Ms. Maya," Jerry interrupts, "but I gotta stop you right there. There's no way I can do that many in just two weeks." I slump against the counter, dejected. I'll resort to begging, if necessary.

"Oh pretty, pretty, please, Jerry!" I plead, keeping the whine out of my voice…mostly. "Couldn't you do it for your favorite Brooklyn girl?"

"It's impossible, Maya," he replies firmly.

"Even for the best engraver in all of the five boroughs?" He laughs then, but I can tell my flattery is softening him up.

"Please, Jer," I said, my tone serious. "You know how much I hate having to decline orders. It's a bad look when you're still trying to build your base. Plus, I think these are for a wedding. If we do the wedding, they could refer us for other weddings, come back for birthday gifts, corporate retreat merch…the possibilities are endless."

"You are tenacious, Ms. Maya, but there's no way I can engrave all those delicate glasses—you know I'll likely break a few in the process—in two weeks. Not if we have to ship them too." Did Jerry just give me a glimmer of hope?! I start pacing again, faster than before.

"So you could do it if we *don't* have to ship them?" I hold my breath and silently pray that puppy dog eyes work over the phone. I slow my pacing while I listen for Jerry's answer.

"Well…I guess if you don't have to ship them, I could finish them by the 26th." I let out a victorious yelp before he continues. "But does that mean you're going to drive them up yourself?" Jerry's skepticism comes through loud and clear. Hand delivering orders is hardly part of my business model, but this one is clearly for a wedding and I tend to go above and beyond for a couple's special day. I'm a true romantic. Based on my Tinder activity, we're a dying breed, at least in the Tri-State area.

"Yeah, Jer. I don't think I have a choice. But hey, I'll make a weekend of it. I haven't been to Cape Cod in maybe…five years?"

"Ok…" he says hesitantly. "My work load isn't too crazy right now. If you're going to drive them, two weeks might be enough time."

"Thank you so, so, *so* much for making this work," I practically shriek. He didn't guarantee the timeline, but that was good enough for me in my desperate state. "I promise this will be the last rush order until Rico is back."

"OK, Ms. Maya. Like I said, I'll do my best," Jerry says, sounding a bit resigned. I breathe a sigh of relief. I don't *love* how he didn't actually commit to a date, but he's also yet to let me down. He's earned the benefit of the doubt. Before disconnecting the call, I ask him to give progress updates as he goes.

I droop against the counter, a little out of breath from pacing so hard. The galette is probably cool enough to eat now, and I've worked up an appetite. I cut a generous slice and swat Khan off the counter before he steps a curious paw into my dessert.

I adopted Khan two years ago when my best girlfriend, Denise, moved to an apartment that doesn't allow pets. Big dogs or loud, yapping dogs, I could understand, but how can a landlord say you can't have cats? How would you even enforce that? Either way, Denise hadn't wanted to risk it.

Before Khan, I never bothered with animals of any kind. It was partly because I didn't want to have to worry about a ding against me in New York's cutthroat apartment scene, partly because pet food is yet another expense, and partly because I worried about getting attached to something that could be gone in a few years. Especially cats, who barely act like they like you most of the time. Before this fluff butt landed in my lap, I thought I was OK on my own.

I fell in love with him as soon as Denise brought him over, of course. Apparently I'd just been depriving myself of the cutest and cheapest therapy available considering my dismal insurance. Though Khan weighs just ten pounds and two thirds of that has got to be hair, –long, black strands which he leaves all over my apartment– he still eats like a giant panther. Lucky for him, I'm willing to pay for purrs and head butts with kitty snacks and premium wet food.

"Sorry, Khan, but mama earned this one. I'll get you some salmon." I reach on top of the fridge for his food and get a can opener from the drawer. One whiff of the salmon pâté and Khan attacks his bowl before I can even get my hand out of the way. If only all men were so easy to please.

I grab a fork from the still open drawer and knock it closed with my hips before settling on the futon next to my craft area. The futon, a small ottoman, and my TV are the only parts of my living room that haven't been swallowed up by my growing craft area. I guess that means business is good!

The first bite of warm peach and buttery pastry hits my tongue and I hum in appreciation. Most people think the secret ingredient is nutmeg but I also add a pinch of cardamom for more complexity. It's not in the recipe, but I prefer to get the basics down and then let improvisation make it great. Nothing rounds out a productive day like a fresh baked dessert.

I take another bite and stare wistfully out the kitchen window. When my grandma passed, I made it my mission to make every recipe in her favorite cookbook as a way to feel close to her. It was a 400-page monster of a book focusing on pastries and bread. Two years later, I finished the book and just kept cooking, clearly addicted. It's now on my always-growing list of hobbies. I've probably made this particular galette at least four times, tweaking the spices until I get it perfect. No doubt my cooking crusade is to blame for my sizable booty, thick thighs, and soft tummy, but if the perfect body means giving up dessert, go ahead and call me "Precious".

I giggle to myself at my silliness and pull my computer into my lap. Score! The buyer is online. I open a chat window and hope this Adam guy is understanding.

APark644

It's_Personal: Hello, Mr. Park.

APark644: Hello. Who is this?

It's_Personal: My name is Maya Davis. I'm reaching out from It's Personal. You just purchased the champagne flutes for Bryan and Jessi right?

APark644: Yeah, that's me. Wow, I didn't realize the site had a chat feature.

It's_Personal: Yes. I hope it's OK I reached out to you.

APark644: It's cool. What's up?

It's_Personal: Unfortunately, due to an error with the site's messaging system, you weren't notified that there is a delay for all engraved items from It's Personal.

APark644: Damn. Do I need to cancel my order?

The back of my neck suddenly feels clammy. *Damn, stupid messaging system!* I allow myself two seconds of panic before taking a deep breath and refocusing on potential solutions.

It's_Personal: Hopefully you don't need to cancel. Is there any flexibility in your dates?

APark644: The event is the evening of June 28th.

It's_Personal: Oh, OK. So no flexibility at all.

APark644: No, sorry.

APark644: Is there anything else in your shop that would be ready sooner?

It's_Personal: What's the occasion?

APark644: It's a super fancy engagement party. 175 people will be there.

It's_Personal: 175 people for an engagement party? Wow. Well, for starters, you may want to order more than 175 flutes, just in case some break in transit.

APark644: Good idea. I hadn't thought of that.

It's_Personal: And as far as something for an upscale event in Cape Cod, those items are all going to take similar amounts of time.

It's_Personal: Or longer.

APark644: Shit.

A chuckle bubbles out of my chest. I wouldn't want to be in his position either.

It's_Personal: LOL.

APark644: Sorry! It's just this was like the only thing they asked me to do for the wedding.

It's_Personal: I was actually reaching out to see if hand delivery of the flutes on the day of event would work. My engraver says he could have these done by June 26th, but that doesn't leave time for shipping.

APark644: Seriously?

Why would I lie about this? How often does this guy receive hand deliveries in Cape Cod?

It's_Personal: Yeah. I just really hate to cancel orders and you're already tight on time.

APark644: Is there an extra fee for hand delivery?

It's_Personal: No. Just consider this my way of saying sorry about the messaging mix-up.

APark644: Thanks so much!!! I'm so glad you could make this work.

APark644: This kind of white glove service will give me something to hold over the rest of the groomsmen! ;)

It's_Personal: LOL!

APark644: Let me double-check with the Maid of Honor about the venue address. Wouldn't want you driving all the way to Cape Cod for nothing.

It's_Personal: Fried clams and a day to walk the beach? I would hardly call that nothing.

APark644: Definitely not. Seafood is my love language.

It's_Personal: OMG. LMAO!

It's_Personal: Mine is pastries.

APark644: Nice!

Am I allowed to flirt with a customer? Technically, he started it.

APark644: Something about chatting is giving me flashbacks to junior high flirting.

APark644: A/S/L?

Oh, this guy must've been a charmer back then. He's plenty smooth now...

It's_Personal: HAHAHA! Well, since you asked...26/F/NYC.

It's_Personal: You?

APark644: 28/M/NYC. What are the odds?

It's_Personal: I'd say pretty high, considering there are like 8 million people living in NYC.

APark644: So we have ourselves a smart aleck, huh?

It's_Personal: Who me?

APark644: OK. Emily just confirmed I got the venue address right, so we're all good. Thanks again.

APark644: In the meantime, PLEASE let me know ASAP if anything else changes. The MOH will literally kill me if I mess this up.

It's_Personal: Will do, Mr. Park. Have a nice night.

Well! That was something. Adam Park not only seems like a reasonable guy, but a super flirty one. The oven's been off for a while, but my cheeks suddenly feel warm. Some men just can't help themselves.

I might need to use this chat feature more often. Too bad that Emily girl had to kill the vibe.

I put away the thread still in bags by the couch and bring up "The Great British Bake Off" on my laptop. Time to binge a few episodes while I knock out the backpacks for the Poughkeepsie High School senior trip.

CHAPTER THREE

Adam

"Custom champagne glasses just for the engagement party? I knew Bryan's family was loaded, but damn!" Cory jokes. He smiles wide around a mouth full of bibimbap and pours himself another glass of soju.

Cory's the youngest of my big brothers, and the biggest bachelor of us all. He doesn't even give the ladies fifteen minutes to cuddle before calling them an Uber, so the idea of basically a mini-wedding before the real wedding is blowing his mind.

It's Sunday, which means all five of the Park men are gathered in the dining room of Mom and Dad's Clinton Hill brownstone for the weekly family dinner. Mom's pulled out all the stops with a traditional Korean dinner this week, probably because Damon—my next oldest brother and a point guard for some team in Portugal—is home for the off-season. He's ignoring Cory in favor of sneaking another helping of tteokbokki.

"It's tacky to talk about money at the dinner table, boys," Dad warns. Dad is definitely old school. He married Mom at twenty-three after just two months of dating. That's not even long enough for your work benefits to kick in these days. He even asked for her dad's permission.

I can't imagine any of my brothers doing that, including the twins, Noah and Henry, Jr. They're the oldest, which supposedly makes them the most responsible—or so Henry, Jr. keeps telling us. He *also* says that one look at the alimony payments his firm secures for their clients is enough to make him swear off marriage forever.

"Sorry, Dad," we all say in unison. Mom and Dad always emphasized the importance of being respectful and having manners. It just never seemed to translate to dating. All five of the Park boys are focused on their careers over women and proud of it, to my mother's great disappointment.

"Money aside, they are having a ton of events," I say in between bites. "There's an engagement party, a bridal shower, and, of course, a bachelor and bachelorette party." Noah gives a low whistle and snatches the last steamed bun before Damon can get it. Damon grumbles to himself as Noah grins triumphantly.

"Then, the week of the wedding, there's going to be a welcome dinner, the rehearsal dinner, *and* a going away brunch after the ceremony and reception." I blow out a sigh, exhausted just talking about it. "It's going to be four days of torture." If Cory and Noah's smiles are any indication, they've got no sympathy for me at all. Dicks.

"You could do with some romance in your life, Adam," my mom says as she adds more kimchi to her bowl. "All of you, actually. Are none of you going to make me a grandma?"

Everyone shifts uncomfortably in their seats. Dad clears his throat and pours himself more soju.

"Leave the boys alone, Marie. Not everyone is lucky enough to have what we have." He leans over and gives her a peck on the cheek, which earns him a blush and a quiet giggle.

"C'mon, Dad," protests Damon. "I'm still sowing my wild oats."

If Mom were any less of a lady, I would swear I saw her roll her eyes.

"Son, you've sown enough oats to give Quaker a run for their money."

The whole table erupts in laughter. Even Dad chuckles to himself after trying to hide his laugh behind a cough. His "dad jokes" have been getting funnier lately, except when they're directed at me, of course.

Noah stands and dings his fork on his wine glass.

"Ahem! I have an announcement to make! Luxe Partners has just added Chris Pang to our client roster!" Mom claps excitedly, while the rest of us look at each other confused. Noah nearly pouts, exasperated by his uncool family.

"Chris Pang?" Continued silence..."The best friend in 'Crazy Rich Asians'?...It was his wedding they all went to in the movie?!" A chorus of "oh"s rings out as recognition dawns on us. Cory just shrugs and starts scrolling on his phone. Not all of

Noah's clients are A-listers, but Luxe Partners' roster has been steadily growing since he joined eight years ago.

While we congratulate our brother, Mom runs to the kitchen and comes back with the bottle of champagne she keeps chilled for such occasions. Dad grabs the glasses from the sideboard and Damon uses the distraction to take the last of the sticky chicken.

"Congrats, baby brother," Henry, Jr. taunts, knowing Noah hates when Henry reminds him he's six minutes older. Noah playfully shoves him before Henry, Jr. flicks his ear and incites roughhousing at the table, a Park family no-no.

"Knock it off, boys!" shouts Dad, immediately putting an end to the fighting. "Noah, congratulations on your new client. Let's all raise a glass!"

Everyone raises their glasses and cheers Noah. Despite the teasing, we're always sure to celebrate one another knowing it's only a matter of time before someone else gets the kudos.

A buzz in my pocket pulls my attention from the Norman Rockwell painting unfolding in front of me. It's a new email.

You have one unread message from It's_Personal!

"I'm going to check upstairs to see if I left my hoodie last week," I say, while scooting away from the table. I doubt anyone heard me over the Knicks vs. Nets debate that always breaks out when Damon's home.

If Dad had his way, my room would be his home office, but since Mom has a soft spot for her youngest and Dad has a soft spot for Mom, my room remains a time capsule from 2016. Overwatch and Final Fantasy XV posters stare back at me from the walls. I plop down on the flannel sheets and open Etsy to see Maya's message.

Hello Mr. Park,

Thank you again for choosing It's Personal for your personalized gift needs! My engraver has confirmed he can do 200 champagne flutes by June 26th. This is 25 more than you ordered which I HIGHLY RECOMMEND to cover all your guests, especially since it doesn't impact the date. There is a fee for the additional flutes but, as discussed, there is no fee for delivery. Please let me know if this change works for you.

Best,
Maya Davis
Owner, It's Personal

She's online! I click on her screen name so we can chat again in real-time.

It's_Personal

APark644: Hey, Maya. Are you online?

Several minutes go by with no response. She probably just left her laptop open. I close the chat window, but it pops back open almost immediately.

It's_Personal

It's_Personal: Hi, Mr. Park. Yes, I'm online. How may I help you?

APark644: First, you have to stop calling me Mr. Park. It's Adam.

It's_Personal: OK. How may I help you…ADAM?

I lean back against my pillows and smile at Maya's snarky reply. A sassy mouth can be so sexy on a woman.

It's_Personal

APark644: That's more like it.

APark644: I just wanted to let you know a) I definitely want to update to 200 glasses, and b) June 26 still works.

It's_Personal: That's great! Thanks so much for being so accommodating.

APark644: No prob. And you're sure they won't be delayed?

It's_Personal: The engraver assured me he could to it by then.

APark644: Thanks. You're really saving my ass.

It's_Personal: Technically you wouldn't be in this mess if my scheduler hadn't malfunctioned.

APark644: Well, still. Thanks.

It's_Personal: You're welcome. I'll keep you updated. Have a good night!

APark644: Good night, Maya.

I sit up and let out a sigh. That wasn't nearly as flirty as the last time we talked, but I still find myself wondering about this Maya woman. *What does she look like? Where in New York does she live?* I'm pretty sure she'd think I'm a creep if I just came right out and asked those things in the middle of buying champagne flutes. Maybe I'm just starved for good conversation; that's hardly on the menu in my late night encounters, unless moans and cuss words count.

She could be a crazy cat lady, but, for whatever reason, I enjoy talking with Maya, even teasing her. Next time, I'll get her to flirt back.

CHAPTER FOUR

Maya

"You're still coming down for the party in two weeks, right?" I do my best to keep my eyes from rolling. How could I possibly forget? It's only the *third time* she's asked about it since she called.

"Yes, Mom," I say, with all the attitude of an angsty teen. Mom sucks her teeth.

"Don't you 'Yes, Mom' me, Maya. Your schedule has been so unpredictable ever since you left Sharp, Smith & Haley." I scream internally, but don't take the bait. I'm actually surprised she made it a whole twenty minutes before criticizing my life choices.

"...OK, OK. I'll drop it," she says, resigned. "I believe in your art, Maya. That's why we paid for Pratt. But I'll never understand why you had to leave Sharp, Smith & Haley to do it. Why be a starving artist?"

"A starving artist wouldn't have hips like mine," I say, with as much sass as I can get away with. "And like I've said before," I begin in a gentler tone, "working both jobs wasn't working. I kept short-changing my art and I was just miserable."

"Fine, fine. I said I'd drop it."

"And yet we had the conversation anyway," I say, with *way more* sass than I can get away with.

"Maya," Mom warns. I get up to pace off my frustration. My mom and I have always had a great relationship, talking almost daily, but leaving a cushy job in finance to start my own business definitely put a strain on things.

"How is the planning going for the big 4-0? Have you found the perfect dress?"

I can practically hear her grin. Gotcha! When it comes to Evelyn Davis, asking about clothes is fool proof way to change the subject. Meanwhile, I always preferred to either make or thrift my clothes.

I listen to her chatter as I straighten up my bedroom. I've got to stop stockpiling water glasses in here!

When she starts describing the *third* dress she bought "just so I can have options", I put the phone on speaker and settle back into my embroidery. I barely need to be here once she gets going.

A pop-up appears on my phone's lock screen.

You have one unread message from APark644!

Huh. I don't have a new update for him. I wonder why he's reaching out. Without thinking, I grab my laptop and navigate to my inbox.

Hey Maya,

Can you please text me at (347) 555-0932 instead of messaging me here? I'm paranoid I'm going to miss an update from you, and I figure you'll need my number anyway for when you drop the flutes off.

This guy has been weird from the start. First, it seems like he's flirting with me. Now he wants me to text him? I guess I *will* need his phone number for delivery, but—

"Maya? Did I lose you?" Shit! I forgot my mom was still on the line.

"No, no. I'm here, Mom. Sorry. I just got an email about an order. Can I call you back?"

"OK, honey." Her disappointment is palpable.

"Sorry, again, Mom. I promise I'll be there for the anniversary party. I'll even come down the day before and help you choose between outfits." She hums her approval. The only thing Evelyn Davis loves more than buying clothes is showing them off.

"Thank you, honey. That sounds fun. Love you!"

"Love you, too, Mom. And say 'hi' to Dad for me."

"Will do, honey. Bye." I fall back against the couch when the phone disconnects. I love her, but my mom is *a lot*.

I pull my computer back onto my lap and bring up Adam's message. If he wants his updates via text instead of the platform, I guess that's cool with me. I punch his number into my phone and hesitate just a few seconds before texting.

There's no reason to be nervous, Maya. He's just a customer...A very flirty customer, but still.

Adam (Champagne Flutes)

Hello, Mr. Park. This is Maya.

Adam (Champagne Flutes): New phone. Who dis?

Adam (Champagne Flutes): Jk. Hi Maya. What's it gonna take for you to call me Adam?

Sorry. It's a force of habit. This is all a bit unusual.

Adam (Champagne Flutes): What's un-usual?

What's unusual? Everything!

My usual engraver is out. The delay message didn't work. I'm hand-delivering the flutes instead of shipping them. And now we're texting instead of using the website.

Adam (Champagne Flutes): Is that OK? I swear I'm not just trying to get your number

Adam (Champagne Flutes): Mostly…

LMAO!

Why would you want my number? You don't even know me

Who's to say I'm not a serial killer?

Adam (Champagne Flutes): Call it a hunch…

A hunch, huh?

Adam (Champagne Flutes): Yeah. My hunch is telling me this is a very inefficient way to find murder victims.

LOL!!! Who could argue with such flawless logic?

Adam (Champagne Flutes): So Ms. Davis has a smart mouth, does she? ;-)

No comment. ;-)

Adam (Champagne Flutes): Anyway, it's a pain to keep the site open all the time.

They have an app…

Adam (Champagne Flutes): Yeah, but like I said, you'll need my number for delivery anyway.

I guess you're right. I'm actually not a fan of having to go back and forth on the platform either.

Adam (Champagne Flutes): Cool. I'm saving you in my phone.

What are you saving me as?

Adam (Champagne Flutes): Are you sure you want to know? ;-)

Uh-oh. Forget I asked.

Adam (Champagne Flutes): LOL, I'm only teasing! You're Maya – Etsy. What am I in your phone?

Adam (Champagne Flutes).

Adam (Champagne Flutes): Not as sexy as I'd hoped, but it works.

Sexy?! OMG! You know, I usually don't talk to customers like this…

Adam (Champagne Flutes): Not even SEXY customers?

LOL, how would I know whether or not you're sexy?

Adam (Champagne Flutes): I'm happy to send a pic.

Adam (Champagne Flutes): Can't guarantee it won't be NSFW, lol

OMG, that's OK. I don't think I wanna start using my online store like Tinder

Adam (Champagne Flutes): What about OKCupid? ;-)

Never in my life have I met such a flirt.

Adam (Champagne Flutes): I'll stop flirting when you stop flirting BACK ;-)

...

Adam (Champagne Flutes): ANYWAY, is the order close to done?

Since last night? LOL.

Adam (Champagne Flutes): Hey, you never know

No, the engraver didn't call me today.

I promise that any time there is an update, I will let you know ASAP.

Adam (Champagne Flutes): Cool.

Adam (Champagne Flutes): You can even text me if you DON'T have an update.

Adam (Champagne Flutes): You know, to help you narrow down potential murder victims

That's so sweet, but not necessary. I hardly ever feel the urge to kill since they released me

j/k lol!

Adam (Champagne Flutes): Or you could just text to talk

What, like "u up?" ;-)

Adam (Champagne Flutes): See? That's YOU flirting! LOL

OMG. Good night, Adam

Adam (Champagne Flutes): Good night, Maya

I put away my phone out of reach to save myself from texting again and slump back on the couch with a sigh. Wow! Talking with customers doesn't usually leave me with such a goofy smile on my face. I hope I have an update for him tomorrow...

CHAPTER FIVE

Adam

The music surrounds me, pounding rhythmically as if this club has a pulse. I watch the dance floor from the safety of the bar and see sweaty bodies gyrating in an obvious mating dance, pushing and pressing against one another, hoping to find a partner, if only for the night. Cory dragged Damon here after he complained that his busy schedule and the language barrier made dating almost impossible while overseas. I tagged along for some bro time, but it's too loud to *think* in here, let alone talk. Cory and Damon don't seem to mind; they're in the center of it all, switching dance partners any time the song changes.

I take a sip of my watered down drink and check my watch. While I'm considering just leaving my brothers to their fun, a big, familiar arm grabs me across the shoulders from behind.

"Don't tell me our baby bro is thinking about calling it a night?" Damon looks like he's just finished playing a quarter of basketball, but the woman boldly curled against his chest doesn't seem to mind. She gives me an approving glance, which I ignore. *Bros before hos.*

"I was thinking about it, yeah. This place is a bit too trendy for me." Cory comes up behind us and shoves his way to sit next to me at the bar.

"Don't give him a hard time, D. You know baby bro can't dance." I roll my eyes and signal the bartender for another round.

"I can too dance. It's Jr. who's got the two left feet." When Henry Jr. moved to Westchester, all women's toes in NYC breathed a sigh of relief. The bartender wordlessly replaces my empty glass with a new Jameson on the rocks. At least the service is good. Cory just smirks.

"So why is the missing member of BTS sitting here sulking at the bar instead of tearing up the dance floor with some babes?" Cory does a few exaggerated boy band dance moves, cracking everyone up. He might be a finance wiz kid, but he's also a huge goofball.

"I haven't found the right girl yet. I prefer to be more strategic before—"

"The right girl?" Cory interrupts. "For what? It's just a dance." For some reason I'm overthinking things tonight and my brothers can tell. Well, Cory can, at least. Damon is pretty busy with his tongue down the bold girl's throat. They're making out uncomfortably close to me, and I'm two seconds from letting them know I didn't agree to a threesome.

"*Like I was saying*," I continue. Cory rolls his eyes dramatically. "Some of us prefer to be more strategic, while others," I look at Cory and Damon pointedly, "seem to be more about quantity over quality." Damon briefly comes up for air. Bold girl is now chewing his gum, and I try not to gag. *Mono, party of two!*

"If you're looking for quality girls, you're in the wrong place." Damon nods to his new "friend". "No offense." She seems to take offense, however, as she walks off in a huff, leaving Damon to chase after her.

"And he just made my point. We came out to hang and now he's going to be chasing after some girl all night." Cory takes a shot and raises his eyebrow.

"No, *you* came out to chill. *We* came out specifically to find some chicks to help Damon with his dry spell. You're more than welcome to fuck off back to Brooklyn if these women aren't to your liking." Cory's being a dick about it, but he has a point. Since when do I stress about the quality of my hookups? I survey the crowd and find a busty brunette dancing sensually by herself. I pound down the rest of my drink and make my way over.

"There you go, baby bro!" Cory shouts after me. "Go see if she's marriage material!" I throw a middle finger up behind me and reach the brunette.

"Hi."

"Hi," she purrs. She looks me up and down before turning to grind her butt against my crotch. *That was easy.*

I put my hands on her hips, guiding her movements. There's no way she doesn't know I'm enjoying myself. Any closer, and we'll need to use protection. When the beat speeds up, she turns to face me, pressing her breasts against my chest. She leans close, purposely letting me feel her lips against my ear.

"I'm glad to see the stereotypes aren't true."

"What?" I ask.

"You know," she says suggestively, and winks for good measure. *No, lady. I really don't.*

"What stereotypes?" She finally stops dancing against me, looking at me like I've grown a second head.

"The stereotypes about Asian men." She winks again and drops her gaze to my dick. "I can tell you're packing some serious hardware."

My jaw drops and I step away from her immediately. The nerve of this bitch! I head back to the bar, opening and closing my fists in frustration. Damon is already there, handing a drink to the bold girl from earlier.

"What's up, man? You look ready to punch a wall." I give him a grim nod and order another drink while I try to cool off.

"A little. The chick I was dancing with said she was glad I have a big dick." I gulp down my swiftly delivered drink and motion for another one. I straighten when I see the anger in Damon's eyes.

"Is my baby bro whipping his dick out on the dance floor? Bonehead move, man." I look at him, thoroughly exasperated.

"What? Hell no. She could just tell from dancing with me." Damon doesn't try to hide his confusion.

"Uh...And that's *bad*?" I gulp the second drink and take a calming breath.

"She said she was glad I had a big dick considering the stereotypes about *Asian men*." At my last words, Damon looks nearly as angry as I am.

"Really, dude? In 2024? Still?"

"Right!" I said, feeling validated. That chick was rude as hell. "It came out of left field and threw me way the fuck off. I barely said two words to her and she's calling me the Ron Jeremy of Asians." Damon coughs into his drink to hide his smile.

"It's not funny, dude." His smile opens up to a full laugh and I start to laugh too. "OK, that was a little funny. But that woman certainly wasn't. In what world is it a good idea to compare someone to their entire race?" Damon turns to me, his face suddenly serious.

"It's ten times worse overseas, bro. It gets so bad sometimes I wonder if it's worth it, just for the BS money I'm getting paid."

"I'm sorry, man. That's awful."

"I'm one person's stereotype, and another person's fetish. All the while, I'm just missing home." I've never heard my brother talk like this.

"Are you thinking about giving it up?" I ask gingerly. We all want Damon home, but we don't want to pressure him. It's his life, after all. He wipes his hand over his face.

"I don't know…," he sighs. "I might not *quit*, but maybe just let my contract run out at the end of next season." Holy shit! My brother is finally coming home. I wondered when he'd be ready. He's in his 30s already, and playing basketball is not a forever job.

"That's major, Damon." He cuts his eyes to me quickly.

"Don't tell Mom or Dad. I don't want to get their hopes up if I change my mind but…I don't think I'll change my mind." He looks so down right now, I feel bad for bringing up the brunette's idiot remark. To be abroad, not looking like those around you or speaking the language? It must be tough.

I get so happy at the thought of having my brother back, just a train ride away, that I forget all about the woman, and buy us a round of drinks instead.

"Your secret's safe with me."

CHAPTER SIX

Maya

I load the last of the glasses into the back of my car and lean on my trunk in relief. I'm already exhausted and I haven't even left; I don't know if I'll survive another rush order with Jerry as long as I live. Though he said he'd be done with the flutes two days ago, he ended up getting a rush order from another client that took priority.

When June 26th came and went, I reached out to Adam with the bad news. He was pretty pissed to say the least, since two days wasn't enough time for him to order new favors from somewhere else. Ever since I dropped that bombshell, I started giving him almost hourly updates. His texts were understandably way less flirty.

After several pleading calls in which I promised him Napoleons from scratch (including the puff pastry), Jerry finally finished Adam's order late last night. As requested, I texted

Adam, even though it was one in the morning. I let him know I'd have to rush over to Jerry's apartment in Staten Island at the crack of dawn before HE left on vacation too—*Am I the only one not taking time off this Summer?*—and I'd head to the venue after my morning class.

Somehow, I let Tiffany talk me into leading crafting classes part-time at her Summer camp in Harlem. No wonder I'm worn out. I've already been to three of the five boroughs and I still have a four-hour drive ahead of me.

When Tiff's program in DC ran out of grant money, I assured her New York had plenty of underserved students in need of support. She linked up with Harlem School of the Arts two weeks later, but found out their usual crafting teacher got married and is taking the Summer to backpack through South America with her new wife.

As Tiff's closest friend in the city since her move, I volunteered, which meant my Saturday mornings lately have been spent waist deep in yarn, popsicle sticks, and construction paper. Tiffany has bought drinks every girls' night to make it up to me but honestly? It's heaven. One of these kids might become a lifelong art lover because of this program. That's how it happened for me, at least.

I see the last of the kids off to the 6 train and check my watch. 12:15pm. I plug the venue address into my phone and head back to the center—my car is parked out front. Google Maps says the drive will take four hours, so if I add an hour for traffic and another thirty minutes for bathroom breaks, I should get there around... 5:00pm. That's cutting it close for an event that starts at 6:30pm.

I double-check the address and hope I've added in enough buffer. Adam is not going to be happy but the situation couldn't be avoided. Maybe he'll have mercy on me because I was helping kids? Not likely. New Yorkers aren't exactly known for their compassion. Hand deliveries are *definitely* not the way to go in the future. They are way too nerve-wracking.

I take a deep breath before writing my text.

Adam (Champagne Flutes): You're not going to get here until 5:00pm?! Emily is going to kill me.

I thought the bride's name was Jessi?

Adam (Champagne Flutes): It is. Emily is the MOH/wedding planner. I told her not to worry because YOU told me not to worry and now we might be screwed.

I'm sorry again, Mr. Park. It was really the perfect storm of events that led to this. But I promise I've built in more than enough travel time.

> **Adam (Champagne Flutes):** I don't really have a choice, do I? And, for the love of God, please call me Adam. No sense being so formal at this point.

> OK... I have to go. I can't text and drive.

I force close my messages and set my Spotify to Chronixx Radio. For long drives, it's gotta be either reggae or Motown classics. Today, Protoje and Kabaka Pyramid keep me company while Google leads the way.

Three hours and one bathroom break later, a call interrupts the chorus of "Eternal Light".

"Hey, Denise." She knows I'm driving otherwise she definitely would have texted.

"Hey, girl! I can't believe you're driving all the way to Cape Cod for some lousy champagne flutes. And you didn't even charge for gas?! What kind of nonsense is that?"

Denise has been my girl since our days at Pratt. We both started in Apparel Design, but I switched to Textiles sophomore year. I've always liked making clothes, but I never had much fashion sense. Denise, on the other hand, interned with Tory Burch and even had her senior project featured at the Fashion Institute in NYC.

Denise has a personality as big as her breasts (DDD), a big booty (she's fond of calling it a 'donk'), and big hair—she's just big all around. She and Tiffany are a lot alike, which is why they bonded immediately when I invited Tiff out for karaoke with us. Unfortunately, now that means I have *two* people busting my balls about my relationship status and my issues with confidence. There's not a day where I don't wish I had the courage to flaunt my "assets" the way they do instead of hiding mine under sweaters and large prints. It's not that I don't want to, but...Ugh, now is *not* the time to spiral.

"OK first of all, my champagne flutes are not lousy. They are beautiful and pair perfectly with a Cape Cod engagement party." I feign annoyance, but from her laughter, I can tell she knows I'm teasing.

"Sorry, girl. I'm just salty I didn't get an invite to this weekend getaway. I like wine. I like lobster. What about me?"

I laugh at her ridiculousness and maneuver a tricky left exit before responding.

"I'm sorry. You know I'm mostly going to be working. After I deliver these flutes to Adam, I'm going to drop my card at a few venues in case they're looking for personalized items for future events."

"Oh it's *Adam* now, is it? Not 'Mr. Park'?" If we were having this conversation face to face, I just know she'd have an eyebrow raised.

"No, no, no. Don't make it like that. I literally tried to call him Mr. Park but he keeps insisting I call him Adam. We've never spoken on the phone. I don't even know what he looks like. There's really nothing there."

"Don't know what he looks like? You didn't even look him up on Facebook or Instagram?" My silence is telling. "Girl! You weren't the least bit curious?" I love Denise, but she can certainly make a mountain out of a molehill.

"I've never looked because he's just a client and this is not 'You've Got Mail' or some other rom-com."

"Not with *that* attitude," Denise scoffs. I roll my eyes.

"I'm a romantic, but I'm also a realist and in *real* life, people don't appreciate when you stalk them on social media."

Denise sucks her teeth and is silent for a moment.

"...What if I look him up for you? Is that still considered stalking?"

I laugh out loud and shake my head. This is why Denise is one of my ride or dies. "I love you, girl, but I gotta go. The exit for the venue is coming up and I don't want to miss it."

"Ok, spoilsport. Love you, too and have a great weekend!"

I take the Chatham exit and pull into the Chatham Bars Inn ten minutes later. As I park my Hyundai Accent next to an *actual Bentley* in the circle drive, I suddenly feel incredibly out of my league. *Just get in and get out, Maya. Deliver the flutes and ignore the cars worth several years' worth of rent.*

A tall, Asian man wearing what I would describe as "J. Crew chic" makes a bee line for me, his mouth in a tight line. This must be Adam. I stay where I am and try not to pull at my oversized cardigan. Adam looks like he just walked out of a catalog, meanwhile I look like a fashion-challenged substitute teacher. *Just perfect!*

"Please tell me you're Maya," he demands. Yep, this is definitely Adam.

"I'm Maya. And I have the flutes." I press my mouth into a nervous smile and extend my hand, but he doesn't take it. I lower it after a few awkward seconds. "I told you I'd make it in time. Luckily there wasn't much traffic."

The whole time I'm talking, he's warily assessing me, from the messy bun of locs on top of my head, to my plaid, pleated skirt, down to my worn out Mary Janes. I can't read his expression, but I'd guess it's impatience that I've got the nerve to still be talking instead of unloading his order. This is the last time I ever give white glove service.

"Yes, you made it on time...Just barely." *Jerk.* "Can I help you carry these in? I wouldn't want an accident at the last moment."

Could this guy be any ruder? I get here thirty minutes earlier than planned after driving 4+ hours and I don't even get a "hello" and a handshake? And now he thinks I'm going to drop his precious cargo on the floor like a complete rookie? Time to wrap this up and check into my room down the road. I grab a load of boxes and incline my head toward the entrance.

"Please lead the way, *Mr. Park.*" It might be petty, but if being formal annoys this jerk, I will *never* call him "Adam". The line of his mouth gets even tighter. Without a word, he picks up the other boxes like they weigh nothing and takes off at a brisk pace, leaving me to awkwardly run-walk behind him to keep up.

I follow him up the stairs, through double doors, and into what seems like a maze of hallways. Everyone we pass is busy, placing flower arrangements, reviewing place settings, lighting candles. From the looks of it, there are at least three other events happening here tonight. It feels like a carefully choreographed ballet and reminds me why I love doing what I do, regardless of the few difficult clients.

We finally reach the Beach House Grill. The color palette is white, pink, and gold with pops of coral. The flowers and chandeliers complete the look that screams "old money". At least the *flutes* will fit in here. I, on the other hand, should head back to my car as soon as possible.

"This place is so beautiful," I whisper, awe clear in my voice. I do a 360 to take it all in, the box still in my hand. "So where should we put these boxes?"

Adam opens his mouth to answer but suddenly a blonde, willowy woman stomps over and steps in between us. She stands a bit too close and levels me with an icy glare.

"Finally! I'm assuming you're here with the champagne flutes?" I nod, too overwhelmed at the hostility coming off this woman in hot waves. "Thank goodness! I was two minutes from talking to the venue manager about a potential Plan B if you didn't show." Her intense gaze doesn't waver as she gestures towards a table to her right.

"Just put them there and Adam and I will worry about set-ting them up." With a flip of her hair and a quick pivot towards the restaurant staff, I consider myself dismissed. This is why I prefer to ship. Safe in my apartment, I can pretend wannabe bridezillas like this don't exist.

I unload the boxes as fast as I can and turn back to Adam who seems to still be watching me. What is this guy's problem? Time to put on a fake smile and get the hell out of dodge.

"Thank you for being so accommodating, *Mr. Park*, and my apologies again for the delay. Delays aren't the norm, and I hope you consider 'It's Personal' for your future personalization needs." While my words say "Ms. Professional", my eyes are saying "Fuck you and your fancy party". I head back to my car without waiting for an answer, though I can feel him watching my back. I won't hold my breath for a five-star review.

CHAPTER SEVEN

Adam

Four hours later and the party's finally winding down. The champagne flutes were a hit, as were the mussels marinara and tiramisu courtesy of Bryan's dad. After dinner, both sets of parents kept the speeches short to get right to the open bar and DJ, and the guests of honor made googly eyes at each other the whole night. Even I have to admit it was a good party, though I'm not sure it was worth $25,000.

I pull off my already loose tie and shove it in the pocket of the suit jacket hanging on the back of my chair. I hate wearing a suit, even if it is linen. Jessi loved Emily's suggestion for the guests to dress in the same colors as the party, so I'd had to buy this stupid suit from Banana Republic at the last minute.

Speaking of Emily, I see her making her way towards me and try to down the last of my bourbon before she can corner me. To say she's been coming on strong this evening would be an understatement. She almost seems a little...off. I pound the empty glass down on bar and rise to leave just seconds too late.

"Adam! Don't tell me you're heading out so soon?" She tries to pull off a sexy pout, but the effect is ruined by her slight slurring from too much champagne. She drapes her hand on my shoulder and toys with the hair on the back of my neck. I look around nervously, because she isn't usually so public with her advances.

"Uh, yeah," I say, grabbing my jacket and putting it on to force her to move her hand. "It's been a long day. I'm totally beat." From how much she's swaying, Emily should probably head back to her hotel room too. I haven't seen her this plastered since...well never.

"Are you gonna be OK, Emily? I think you've had too much to drink." She rolls her eyes before suddenly pounding a fist on the bar. A few people nearby hurry back to the dance floor to avoid the scene unfolding and I start to worry whether I'll ever get back to my room. The bartender sends me a look of sympathy before making himself busy on the other side of the bar.

"I can't *believe* that woman from earlier!"

"What woman?" I whisper, willing her to lower her voice as well.

"The woman with the champagne flutes. From 'It's Personal'?" I knew she was talking about Maya before I even asked. For some reason, Emily has been extra wound up since they ran into one another. Sure, she'd cut it close, but Maya hadn't actually been *late*. Maybe Emily needed a vacation if she was *that* on edge about something so minor.

She's eyeing me now, like everything I'm thinking is written all over my face. Hell, maybe it is. It's been a long night.

"You think I'm overreacting, don't you?" I shrug one shoulder.

"Experience has taught me never to say that to a woman." Emily practically sneers at me.

"Always so smooth. Don't think I didn't see you checking her out, Mr. Smooth." I step back, removing her hand from where it's been resting on my forearm. She sways a bit more.

"Is that your type? Instead of elegant, polished, and successful," *like me*, she silently finishes, "you want some fat craft lady who can barely meet her own deadlines?"

"Emily, I don't know what's gotten into you, but it's not a good look. The flutes were a hit and the party was a success. I'm heading to bed, and you might want to call it a night too. Sleep off whatever it is that's going on with you."

Emily's eyes go glassy with hurt and embarrassment before she quickly feigns indifference and heads back onto the dance floor with a flip of her hair. I head towards the elevator, now painfully aware that a more direct conversation with Emily is in order.

I sink down into the plush sofa in front of the fireplace. The suite is beyond luxurious, with a 60" flatscreen, a window seat overlooking the water, and 1000 thread count sheets on the king size bed. Away from the noise of the party, I finally have the quiet and headspace to think about the woman who caught my attention earlier: Maya.

Who knew someone that cute was on the other end of the computer this whole time? She showed up with a killer smile, a plump little ass, and big brown eyes like a deer, or a Disney princess. Her hair was in one of those messy buns girls love, but I could tell hers was long, maybe all the way down her back. Despite the gray cardigan that did nothing for her hourglass figure, I could see she was also hiding a great pair of tits. Mmmmm. A model would fall over with breasts like that.

I start getting a hard-on just thinking about her and lazily rub myself through my pants. She was voluptuous, but it was her eyes that hit me square in the chest, even across the parking lot. I knew it was her when she pulled up, looking like a lost lamb. *I'll be your big, bad, wolf any day, baby!*

I lean back and let my mind wander, remembering how her eyes widened when she saw me. Maybe she felt it too, that crazy connection. A connection that left me, a guy who's normally "Mr. Charming" completely speechless. Like an idiot, I just stood there, gaping at her. The moment I saw her, I couldn't help but imagine getting her alone so we could...get to know each other better.

Not that I let on. *Mr. Smooth*, as Emily called me earlier, would never admit he liked a woman he'd just met. That would come off as *way* too thirsty. But judging by the glare on Maya's face when she sprinted out of here earlier, I may have overcorrected.

I should've invited her to the party, maybe asked her to dance. It would've been the perfect excuse to get close to her, put my hands on her body. I'd press myself against her and whisper all the hot things I wanted to do to her until she suggested we head back to my room. Then she'd be here with me now instead of wherever she ran off to when Emily showed up. Now I'm stuck jerking off in my hotel room like a pervert.

I breathe deeply and enjoy the sensations building in my balls. She probably smells good too, like vanilla or roses or something. I should've hugged her when she arrived. She drove all that way and then I didn't even shake her hand? God, she must've thought I was a total jerk. If I'd hugged her, not only would I know for sure whether she smells as incredible as she looks, but I also would've gotten to feel those luscious looking breasts pressed against my chest.

I groan thinking about all opportunities I missed with Maya. If she'd stayed, we definitely would've danced, and my hands would've ventured lower, down to that plump backside I barely got a glimpse of. Just from that glimpse, I could tell she has more than enough to grab onto under that hot skirt of hers. It almost didn't cover her ass, especially when she bent down to get those boxes. Just a glimpse had me tongue tied the whole way to the banquet room. If she came up for drinks, maybe she would've let me put my hand on her knee to see how soft her skin is. If it's half as soft as it looked, I'd be in trouble.

I slip my hand inside my slacks now and start stroking more purposefully. Her lips were full and pink. I imagine them parted and out of breath from the feel of my hand caressing her leg. I'd inch up higher and higher until I reached the apex of her thighs. I would tease her through her panties, feeling her wetness against my hands, until she sighed my name, the waves of her orgasm crashing down on her.

Satisfied and still breathless, those eyes of hers would turn molten as she dropped to her knees to take me in her mouth. I bet those lips would look great wrapped around my dick. I would lean back while she catered to me, licking every inch of my hard length as I pulled out that messy bun to see just how long her hair really is.

She called me "Mr. Park"...*Again*. If I'd been nicer to her, I could see if she still called me "Mr. Park" when I bit her shoulder while pulling down her bra strap. Would she still be so formal if I unsnapped her bra and sucked and caressed her dark brown nipples? Would she finally call me "Adam" if I nudged those thighs apart and pushed into her hot center until she screamed my name?

"Fuck!" I grunt as I cum in my pants like a teenager. I hated these pants anyway. I pull them off, along with my boxers, and head to the shower, resolving to apologize tomorrow and get to know Maya a little better.

CHAPTER EIGHT

Maya

A stream of sunlight breaks through the crack in my curtains and hits me right in the face. I knew I should've brought my sleep mask. Half of my pillows are on the ground and my left leg is tangled in the sheets. I slept horribly.

It could have been my room, which was clean but looked like it hadn't been updated in decades and came complete with paisley wallpaper and a hammock chair hanging from the ceiling. It could have been the nonexistent water pressure or the two-ply sheets which resembled toilet paper. My hotel falls quite a few stars short of what I'm guessing is available at the Chatham Bars Inn.

More likely, however, was that I was still a bit shaken from yesterday. After checking into my room, I called Denise back and told her all the juicy details, from showing up woefully underdressed, to being scolded by some blonde bimbo that must've been Adam's girlfriend. And that dick had the nerve to flirt with me!

After she was sufficiently appalled when she heard about "Ms. Plan B", and even threatened to drive up just to "beat her ass", we laughed about the state of my room until she had to leave for her kickboxing class. According to her, it sounded like Scatman Crothers' room in "The Shining". All it needed was a poster of Cleopatra Jones over the bed and a lava lamp.

I did leave a few things about yesterday out, though, like how hot Adam was, or how even though he didn't shake my hand, he stared at me the whole time. He seemed to be silently sizing me up. For what, I don't know. If I hadn't felt so out of my depth, I might've snuck a few glances myself. I snuggle deeper into the bed, trying to convince myself the sheets aren't scratchy and the pillows aren't lumpy.

Thinking about him now, his good looks were almost dangerous. Dark hair just long enough to brush his eyebrows and fall around his ears. Deep, nearly black eyes that made me nervous with their close scrutiny. A full, sensual mouth I could see even through his frown. Shoulders broad enough to be a comic book hero.

And the rest of him? Well, he clearly spends his free time in the gym or running instead of making blackberry cobbler like me. I could see his muscles subtly flex beneath his clothes as he walked (more like stalked) towards me, his well-defined abs apparent even under his dress shirt. I felt like he was crowding me just by standing next to me, looming a good six inches taller than my 5 foot 5 frame.

Men who look like Adam don't usually spare me a second glance, so his quiet, undivided attention had been unsettling. If he'd been just a little less good looking, I would guess he was into me. But that doesn't happen anywhere except my private fantasies. Fantasies where those midnight eyes promise pleasure as they rake up and down my body. He sprinkles light kisses on my lips, my cheeks, my neck, then across my chest, giving a bite to each nipple before soothing them with a warm, wet suck.

I notice what I'm doing, my hand cupping my aching breast thinking of him. A peek at the bedside radio tells me I have time for a "sneaky tweak" before checkout. I won't be able to canvas effectively if I'm too worked up. I lay back and imagine Adam going lower still, his delicious mouth cracking into a mischievous grin as he reaches my round tummy, hooking both thumbs into the sides of my panties.

Justin, my ex, never went down on me. He always said eating out was for men with no stroke game. I didn't have the heart to tell him that meant he should be eating me out daily. He was an accountant, specializing in due diligence for mergers and acquisitions. Despite never forgetting my birthday and bringing me flowers once a month like clockwork, he had all the sex appeal of a guidance counselor. I wasn't broken up when his work had taken him overseas. Maybe if my g-spot had been a tax error, he would have found it.

Something tells me Adam doesn't have that issue. I kick the tangled sheets off and imagine him inhaling deeply between my thighs to smell my essence, nuzzling my clit with his nose before biting down through the fabric. Wow! Thank goodness that mouth can do more than frown at me.

I haven't been this wet maybe ever, my fingers sliding around with ease as I spread the juices flowing from my feminine folds. I'm close now, breathless as I imagine him tugging my panties down, firmly kissing my mound before placing a tentative lick against my womanhood. I jerk up in pleasure and his grin turns positively wicked. He pushes my legs wider, his lips inches from my dripping pussy, and finally...

Buzz buzz buzz...buzz buzz buzz.

Seriously?! Can't a lady have a few minutes to blow off some steam before starting her day? I yank my hand out of my panties and check the display on the offending mobile device.

Adam (Champagne Flutes)

What the hell? He's never called before! I blush as if he could somehow know what I was doing just seconds ago, and wipe my hand on the sheets before answering.

"H-Hello? Mr. Park?" He laughs a low, sexy laugh.

"I thought I asked you to call me 'Adam'. Did I catch you in the middle of something? You seem a little out of breath." If my skin were any lighter, I'd be bright red all over from blushing so hard. I clear my throat and try to sound put together. Surely I can manage that for a quick client call.

"Um, no, no! I was just...packing up since I'm about to check out of my hotel."

There's a pause and I wonder if the call got disconnected.

"Hello? Did I lose you?"

"No, I'm still here," he says tentatively. "I'm just surprised you're still in the area. I thought you'd be back in the city by now."

"Driving at night isn't my favorite, so I decided to stay and check out a few venues in the area."

More silence. Why did he call if he wasn't going to talk?

"So...Was there a problem with the flutes?" I ask, eager to wrap up the world's most awkward conversation.

"The favors were a hit. I, uh...I was actually calling to apologize for my rudeness yesterday. I'm normally more charming, I promise."

I'm even more confused now, because Adam sounds downright *nervous*. And this is the first time a client has ever called to apologize, though I also don't normally give out my phone number. I'm not sure how to respond.

"Uh, it's fine. Don't worry about it."

"No, it's *not* fine," he says more firmly. "That's why I called."

"OK...Well...Apology accepted," I say. I can hear movement, like he's shifting in his chair.

"I was hoping...since you're still around...maybe I could make it up to you with a coffee before you head out?...Or lunch? If you have time." He clears his throat, obviously nervous now. Could this be the return of "Flirty Adam"? I don't answer right away, and he quickly backpedals.

"It's no big deal, really. I just know my Mom would have my butt if she knew I didn't at least offer after you drove all this way." That gets a chuckle out of me and I soften towards this chivalrous near-stranger.

"Ok," I reply. "I guess I have to eat."

We set a time and a place before disconnecting. What do I wear to breakfast with the leading man in one of my steamiest fantasies?

CHAPTER NINE

Adam

I arrive ten minutes before Maya and I are scheduled to meet to ensure we get a good table and to calm my nerves. I can't afford to freeze again when I specifically invited her to breakfast.

Maya shows up to the beachfront restaurant wearing a navy skirt that twirls around her generous hips when she walks. She wears a cream top that hugs her breasts and threatens to turn me into Slick Joe McWolf drooling over Red Hot Riding Hood. The gray cardigan from yesterday is gone, and her ample cleavage tests my ability to maintain eye contact. As she gets closer, I can see that her skirt actually has tiny white ship anchors on it to match her shirt. She's got her hair half up-half down today, and I'm pleased to see it reaches all the way to her ample bottom. I wipe my hands on my khaki board shorts before offering my hand.

"Does that mean you'll shake my hand today?" she asks, though I can tell by the glint in her eyes that she's mostly teasing. I smile sheepishly and pull her chair out before sitting down.

"Yeah. Again, I'm sorry about that. I was just..." *caught off guard*, I finish silently. "I mean, I just didn't want to let Bryan down. I've known him forever but I was still surprised he picked me as his best man. This wedding stuff is hardly my forte." That was actually the truth. She smiles and grabs the menu and I'm relieved I don't have to keep groveling...though I totally would if it looked like she was going to leave.

"So any wedding bells for you and the blonde?" She scoots her chair closer to the table and I nearly go cross-eyed trying to avoid watching her breasts jiggle with the movement.

"Who?"

Maya pauses from reading her menu, her expression curious.

"I thought you might be with the blonde from yesterday. The wedding planner?"

"Oh my God! No. That's Emily. She's the wedding planner, but we're not together. Bryan would kill me."

Maya shrugs and picks back up her menu. How could she think I had a girlfriend after all that flirting before? Hmmm...Actually, I guess there is no shortage of cheaters in NYC, but that's not my style.

Is she single too? I don't see a ring, but she could still be with someone. What kind of boyfriend would let his girl spend the weekend alone in Cape Cod?

"What about you?" Maya looks up from her menu.

"What about me, what?"

"Are you seeing anyone?" I'm so glad I don't sound as nervous as I feel Her eyes dart up from the menu in shock.

"Me?" she practically squeaks.

"Yes," I say, enjoying that I seem to be effecting her too. She plasters on a smile to try to cover her reaction to me.

"No, no one special. Just me and my cat, Khan." *Thank God!* I grin before finally perusing the menu. I can see her squirm in her chair out of the corner of my eye.

"Anyway, it's really OK about yesterday. Trust me, you are definitely not the rudest customer I've ever dealt with." *Ouch!* That's quite the low bar. "You can make it up to me by…" she scans the menu, quickly spotting her choice. "…buying me a pain au chocolat with a side of bacon and a chai tea with oat milk." She puts her menu at the empty place setting beside us and I'm glad she's so decisive. Taking forever to order is one of my pet peeves.

I give the waiter our order when he comes by and try not to stare at Maya. Her cheeks are flushed with color and today, she's wearing gloss that makes her lips look even more kissable. I take a drink of my ice water and try to compose myself. I've never had this reaction to a woman, so I'm a little out of my depth. Since when am I at a loss for words?

"You sure knew what you wanted," I say, because it's the best I can come up with. My brain's been buffering since she sat down. She turns and looks me directly in the eyes. Suddenly my throat is made of sandpaper and I reach for my water glass again.

"I've always been like that. Besides, what's the worst that could happen if you choose wrong? It's one meal out of thousands." She smiles and goes back to looking at the water. "God, what a view! Something about the water and the breeze just relaxes me every time."

I briefly glance at the waves before sneaking another look at Maya.

"Yeah. The view is surprisingly beautiful." She hums her agreement, still soaking in the scenery. Who would bother looking at the beach with her sitting here? We could be on the moon for all I know.

"Do you come to Cape Cod a lot?"

"Oh no," she laughs, like her vacationing on the Cape is somehow ridiculous. "I've been here a total of three times my entire life, including right now. My college roommate threw a couple parties at her parents' place when they were out of town, but those ended when a senior blew chunks on the pool table. Ruined it for everyone." She giggles at the memory and the waiter discretely brings our food and disappears.

"How about you?" she asks as she daintily picks up a piece of bacon to keep her fingers from getting oily. It's something my mom would do, though I push further comparisons between her and my mom out of my head as quickly as possible.

"Nah, not really. This is only my second time and the last time was for another friend's wedding."

We eat in silence for a while, enjoying the beach views and sounds. I clumsily drop my spoon on the ground and when I reach down to pick it up, I see that the ocean breeze Maya loves so much has pushed her skirt up higher on her thighs. Nope, looking at that is *not* going to help me right now. I shift in my seat, trying to discretely hide my arousal.

"So you live in the city, right?" She nods and closes her eyes briefly to savor her pastry. God, to be a pastry! "Where?"

"I live in Fort Greene, not far from BAM," she says.

"Oh cool." *'Cool?' Really?* "I live in Bushwick. I'm from Clinton Hill; my parents still have a place there. But I got my own place once I finished school."

"And where'd you go?"

"Stanford." Pause for applause.

"Wow. That's impressive." She sips her tea and I notice the silences between us are becoming less awkward.

"What about you?" I ask so I don't seem like I'm bragging.

"Where am I from or where did I go to school?"

"Both," I say, surprised that I actually want to know the answer. Conversation was rarely a part of my past relationships, if you can even call them "relationships" when I didn't always know their last name.

"I'm from Washington, DC. I went to Pratt and fell in love with Brooklyn, so I stayed." She shrugs before licking her pinky and using the moistened fingertip to clean the crumbs from her plate. She doesn't seem to be *trying* to turn me on, but still she is, just by being herself. I'm kinda digging how easy her whole demeanor is.

I look down and realize we've finished our meal. Shit. That went by faster than I wanted. The waiter comes by with the check before I can try to stall by ordering more food. Maya takes her purse out and starts digging for her phone. Time for a Hail Mary.

"Is there any way I can bum a ride from you back to the city?" She looks at me doubtfully and I don't blame her. Four hours with a total stranger is not really the norm.

"Um..." I can practically hear her coming to the same conclusion.

"Look, I swear I'm not a psycho," *Yikes!* "I carpooled here with one of the bridesmaids and I'm not sure I can take another long car ride with her." I can see Maya softening, so I continue my pitch.

"I have a ton of work emails to answer," I beg, even clasping my fingers together. "You won't even know I'm there and I will pay for gas." I give her the smile I normally reserve for my hookups and I can see she's a goner. It's almost unfair, but it had to be done.

"Well, if you'll pay for gas *and* snacks, I guess it's OK." She smiles tentatively and then suddenly remembers something.

"Wait a minute! I still have to drop my promo kits around. If you want a ride, you'll have to wait until like noon. Is that still cool?"

"Deal," I say, and hide my intense relief by checking the time on my watch. "Should we meet up back at the Chatham Bars Inn?"

"Sure," she says, hiking up her purse on her arm. She looks back over her shoulder and gives me a wide smile. "Text, if anything."

CHAPTER TEN

Maya

What was I thinking saying yes to a ride back to Brooklyn? I barely know this man other than that he's got great taste in glassware, and his manners go out the window when he's stressed.

The hopeful smile he gave me when I got to the hotel lobby was enough to melt me into a horny puddle. He's just so...hot! And apparently single. And maybe...into me?

After we packed up the car, I texted a picture of Adam's state ID to Denise and turned on Find My Friends so she knows I'm not murdered in a ditch. Or, if I am, she at least knows where the ditch is. Adam doesn't give me serial killer vibes, though, and I'm usually a good judge of character. I should be after fifteen seasons of "Criminal Minds". He also seems pretty desperate to get away from that bridesmaid. What happened on the car ride up? I wonder if it was "Ms. Plan B" from yesterday.

Just like yesterday, I felt him watching me all through breakfast, though I pretended not to notice. I figure that means I'm
entitled to a few peeks during our long ride home. This close,
he's even more handsome than I noticed yesterday, with a light
five o'clock shadow on a jawline so strong it could cut glass. He's
also more muscular than he seemed before; with the two of us
in here, my Accent feels like a clown car.

Two hours in and he's had his nose in his phone for most of the
drive, presumably answering work emails as promised. He has
yet to complain about my Spotify choices, and he paid for the
gas and my requisite Coke Zero and Salsa Verde Doritos when
we stopped in Cranston. Even still, it's unnerving being so close
to him in such a small space. I'm hoping we won't have to stop
again until New Haven (keeping my cool next to him is nerve
wracking!), but that Coke Zero may have other plans.

As he scrolls through his phone, I notice his fingers are long
and defined, like a pianist's. His touches are light and delicate
and each tap results in a flex that makes his shirtsleeves tight
against his forearms. And he asked if I was single...

In the background, Bob Marley serenades about waiting in
vain for love and my skin actually starts to feel hot. I move to
reposition my A/C vent to hit me more directly right when he
reaches to turn up the volume and our hands touch. It feels like

a shock of static electricity travels up my arm and I immediately yank my hand back, laughing nervously. I'm almost positive his cheeks are pinker than they were before.

"Sorry. I just really love this song," he says softly. I check that both of his hands are safely on his side of the car before reaching out to turn the music louder.

"Really? I never would have guessed that," *but I'm glad, because it's one of my favorite songs of all time*. He puts his phone down and turns his body towards mine. I feel a bead of sweat forming in my cleavage.

"Never? Why not?" *Yeah, Maya. Why not?* I struggle for an explanation that doesn't sound like an insult.

"You just seem so…um…contemporary? Like you'd see the latest bands playing in Williamsburg before you would jam out to a classic like 'Waiting in Vain'." He's giving me the full wattage of his smile now, a teasing twinkle in his eye.

"Are you…calling me a hipster?" He playfully pushes my arm and I ignore the second zing of electricity between us. "How dare you!"

Pretending confidence I don't feel, I do my best to flirt back.

"Not a hipster per se, just someone who maybe owns more than one fedora." He laughs out loud now and again pushes my arm playfully. Any more shocks and we're likely to have an accident.

"Ugh! You take that back."

"No can do. I call 'em like I see 'em." Adam sits back in his seat and pretends to pout.

"So we're judging books by their covers now, are we?" I can hear the challenge in his voice and I can't help but take the bait.

"Why? What would you assume about me just from looking at me?"

Now that I've given him permission, he openly devours me with his eyes. I will my nipples not to harden under his gaze, but between the slight chill from the A/C, my form-fitting top, and the Korean heartthrob less than a foot away, I don't stand a chance. I notice Adam's eye twitch.

"Hmmm. I would guess that you like Erykah Badu, India.Arie, and maybe Maxwell."

"That's not fair!" I protest. "We've been listening to my playlist the whole time. You didn't even have to guess."

"Sounds like you're saying I got it right." He folds his arms in smug triumph.

"What about something *not* related to music? What do my looks say about me?"

This time, he goes quiet and considers me in earnest.

"Are you a good cook?" My mouth literally drops open at the accuracy.

"How could you possibly know that?" *Hopefully it's not just the size of my backside.*

"At breakfast, I saw that you really savor food. And you just give off this...homey vibe."

My cheeks warm at the compliment, and I am grateful I can look at the road instead of at his intense eyes.

"Thank you. It's not exactly the most sexy description, but it is accurate."

"'Sexy' depends on who's looking," he says, and I feel his eyes on me before he returns to his emails.

Things remain playful and flirty for the rest of the car ride. I tease him about his taste in music (despite agreeing with most of his choices) and he pretends to be offended and finds some way to touch me with those strong hands of his. Before I pass out in a sweaty, horny heap, we arrive at his place in Bushwick; a gray, three-floor walkup across from a 24/7 deli. For no reason at all, I make a mental note of his address.

He steps onto the sidewalk when I park and I get out too, not quite sure of the protocol. This wasn't a date, right? This is his place, so there's no reason to walk him to the door. I definitely feel nervous like at the end of a date. I'm also amazed I pulled off flirting for so long.

I walk around to his side of the car and extend my hand for a shake goodbye. He surprises me by pulling me in for a strong hug instead. I feel his hard body against mine and hope he doesn't notice I'm shaking with nerves.

"Thanks so much for the ride. You have no idea how much you saved me," he says, so close to my ear I can feel his breath.

He gives a final squeeze before letting me go and I'm glad to be already leaning against the car.

"No problem at all," I say breathily, suddenly having trouble making eye contact.

"Well…" Adam seems just as unsure as me about what to do next. Maybe I should have stayed in the car. I plaster a bright smile on my face and start walking back to the driver's side.

"G'night, Adam. Thanks for being such a great road trip buddy!" Mortified by the word vomit that just spilled out of my mouth, I smile even wider and actually wave before stepping into my car. *Kill me now.*

As I pull away from the curb, I can see Adam in my rearview mirror, and he has the nerve to look amused.

CHAPTER ELEVEN

Adam

I feel a few bones pop as I do a full body stretch in bed. The sheets are that perfect warm from sleep and I rub my legs against them, not quite ready to get up this morning. Then I smile to myself remembering that Maya definitely likes me. Nothing else could explain her mad dash to the car when I was clearly working up the nerve to kiss her. It's probably for the best that she ran away. After all that verbal foreplay, I doubt I would've been able to stop at just a kiss. At least I got to watch her cute little ass shake as she practically bolted to the car.

Maya is different from the women I usually go for in so many ways. For one, she is hardly a size four, but if my almost constant erection on the drive home is any indication, her size isn't a problem. I've also never dated a Black woman before, though there has been attraction in the past. When they showed "Love Jones" at the student union, my crush on Nia Long was instantaneous. Lastly, she seemed almost surprised I was interested. Once a woman knows I want her, she's usually grabbing for my belt buckle or inviting herself up for the night. Running away is a first.

I head to the bathroom to brush my teeth and shower, the whole time thinking about how to engineer more time with her. Ordering a bunch of things from her store is probably coming on too strong, and I think Emily would kill me if I hired Maya again after what she called "the flute fiasco". Can't I just text her at this point? Do I really need a reason? I look at the clock over my dresser and realize I'd better save this for later or I'm gonna be late.

At lunch, Eric almost chokes on his sandwich after hearing about my eventful weekend.

"The Emily situation is getting out of hand. Women think 'no means no' only applies to them."

I moodily chew my sandwich, annoyed he's right.

"Her drunken proposition was after the car ride up where she kept 'accidentally' putting her hand on my leg instead of the gearshift. She supposedly needed my help to change when we got to the hotel too, and then kept offering me booze from the minibar." Eric looks sympathetic.

"I always thought I'd like an aggressive woman, but it sounds terrible the way you tell it. What about the shy one? Mia?"

"Maya," I correct him. "And what about her?"

"Well, since when are you scared to make a move? You had an opening for some 'nighttime fun',"—he emphasizes "nighttime fun" with an obscene hand gesture—"and you missed it."

"My timing was just off. She's different from my usual hookup. I couldn't just drag her into my apartment and send her home in an Uber. I think I might ask her out on a real date." Eric pretends to have a heart attack, clutching his chest, and I feel even more embarrassed.

"Adam Park?! Go on a *date*?!" *OK, wiseass.* "But I'm supposed to be living the single life vicariously through you!"

Once again, Eric is right. This has been our arrangement since we both started at CloudTech three years ago. I amaze him with tales of NYC nightlife, and, in exchange, he bores me to death with seemingly endless pictures of soccer games, cello recitals, gymnastics competitions, and Disney vacations. It's like the guy looked up "family man" in the dictionary and said, "I'll take one of each, please!" He's even got the dad bod to match, courtesy of elementary school bake sales, World's Finest Chocolate fundraisers, and a wife who prefers home cooking over GrubHub.

"Whoa, whoa, whoa. I'm still single. I'm just talking about a date," I say. I should've known Eric would get ahead of himself. As much as he likes my stories, I think he secretly would love to have someone else going through the same family stuff.

"Adam, as long as I've known you, I don't think I've ever heard you talk about a real date. Do you even know what a date is?" I put my drink down and pretend to take notes. This asshole is *loving* having something to hold over my head.

"A date," he says in the most patronizing voice possible, "is when a man and a woman meet at an arranged place and time to do something fun. Most people do dinner, some people do drinks, and some people do something more original."

I roll my eyes and pretend to turn an imaginary page when he continues.

"If the date goes well, you might get a chance for a kiss at the end, or a second date." I close my fake notebook and throw a piece of bread at him to wipe the sarcastic grin off his face.

"Alrighty then." I get up to clear my tray, smiling the whole time. "Back to the salt mines for me. Thanks for being no help whatsoever."

Eric tips an invisible hat at me and I chuckle on the way back to my desk.

In the privacy of my office, I pull out my phone to check out Maya's socials. I know I'm stalling, but I'm also legitimately curious about her.

It's_Personal on Instagram is just a bunch of pics of her products. She's got everything from jewelry, to t-shirts, to canvas bags, to mugs. She even partners with a distillery for personalized spirits. It's_Personal on Facebook and LinkedIn are more of the same. Maybe her personal socials have more details.

There is no "Maya Davis" on Facebook or TikTok. I didn't see her snapping selfies or regularly checking her notifications, so that doesn't surprise me. She has a Pinterest board, but it's just inspiration for her crafts (art supplies, clothing patterns), dessert recipes (I knew she could cook), and cute animal pictures. So far, she doesn't have anything revealing online.

I hit the jackpot with Instagram. MDavis_98 follows It's_Personal and an account for Pratt alums. Her feed features shots of her cooking and eating food, plus reels of her making pottery or snuggling with Khan. There are no pictures of her with a guy since February, so it looks like she really is single. She's never in a swimsuit or arching her back for a thirst trap (unfortunately), but she looks genuinely happy and fun to hang out with.

I open the message app and start texting. I won't miss an opportunity with her again.

CHAPTER TWELVE

Maya

A faint ding sounds from my phone. I look around at my messy apartment; it's starting to look like a hoarder lives here. After rifling through the hoops and canvases all over my couch, I find my phone lying face down in a bag of thread.

Adam (Champagne Flutes)

Adam (Champagne Flutes): Hey there.

Adam is texting me? That can't be right. I must have fallen asleep while doing needlepoint again because there's no way Adam would text me after last night's debacle.

I cringe remembering that I actually *waved* before sprinting to my car. He stood in front of his apartment and watched me drive off with a big grin on his face and, because God's got jokes, I then had to wait at the red light at the end of his block. I could still see the laughter in his eyes in my rearview mirror. I bet he and his friends have already had a good laugh at how ridiculous I am.

Adam had only gotten hotter the more time I spent with him. I found out he's got a great sense of humor, he's smart, and we like the same music. Then, after hours of semi-successful flirting, I freaked out and called him my "road trip buddy". Ugh! You can hardly blame me for running after that.

I throw the blanket off my lap, phone gripped tightly in my hand. No matter how hard I blink, the message doesn't change. Either I'm still sleeping or Adam actually texted me. If Adam really did text me, what do I say? Why would he be texting? I start pacing rapidly until the obvious occurs to me: He probably just left something in my car.

Adam (Champagne Flutes)

Hi there.

Adam (Champagne Flutes): So, thanks again for the ride, Maya. You really saved me.

Not a problem at all, Mr. Park.

Just kidding, LOL

Adam (Champagne Flutes): lol, I was about to say! If you can't use my first name by now

LOL, I was only teasing

Adam (Champagne Flutes): Oh, so you're a tease? … Interesting, lol.

Can Adam ever *not* flirt? My goodness! It's like our car ride unlocked some sort of frisky gene.

Adam (Champagne Flutes)

OMG, I didn't mean it like that!

Sure you didn't, lol

ANYWAY, lol. Did you forget something?

Adam (Champagne Flutes): Forget something?

Yeah, in my car. I'm assuming that's why you're texting?

Adam (Champagne Flutes): …Something like that.

I stop pacing and look at my phone, a little confused.

Adam (Champagne Flutes)

What does that mean, lol?

Adam (Champagne Flutes): I didn't forget something so much as ran out of time.

Adam (Champagne Flutes): To be fair, you DID run away, lol

I can't believe he would bring that up! So much for thinking he is a gentleman.

Adam (Champagne Flutes)

I did NOT run away!

Adam (Champagne Flutes): The skid marks on the sidewalk in front of my apartment beg to differ.

Oh my God! You are such a jerk.

Adam (Champagne Flutes): LOL

So what did you run out of time to do, anyway?

Adam (Champagne Flutes): You really don't know? Or are you just playing coy?

I really don't know. And I couldn't "play it coy" if I tried, lol.

Adam (Champagne Flutes): I was going to kiss you, silly!

Adam (Champagne Flutes): I was actually going to kiss you silly, LOL. Isn't that customary at the end of a first date?

What?! Here I am thinking he was trying to let me down easy when he wanted to *kiss* me? My apartment suddenly feels about 150°F.

Adam (Champagne Flutes)

Yesterday was a date?

Adam (Champagne Flutes): It certainly felt like it to me…Unless that was someone else I was flirting with all the way back from Cape Cod.

Make that 200°F. My face must look like a strawberry at this point. I take off my now sweaty cardigan.

Oh shit. He *was* flirting yesterday. I can't help but pace now, filled with nervous energy. Is Adam, like, into me?

Eeek! I'm practically jogging now. Adam is approximately 300% hotter than any guy I've ever dated. Since when do guys like him wanna go out with girls like me?

Adam (Champagne Flutes)

Just to be clear, you mean free for a date, right?

Adam (Champagne Flutes): Actually I was hoping for another ride.

Adam (Champagne Flutes): That was a joke, BTW. Yes, I meant a date.

Adam (Champagne Flutes): I'll make it REALLY clear it's a date this time ;)

Ohmygod, ohmygod, ohmygod!!!

Adam (Champagne Flutes)

Ha ha. Sure. That sounds great. Where should I meet you?

Adam (Champagne Flutes): Have you heard of Honey's? It's this cool little cocktail bar, and they do mead and small plates

> Mead, huh?

Adam (Champagne Flutes): Yup. Feel like pretending to be a viking with me?

> LOL! I'm down

Adam (Champagne Flutes): Great. I'll see you then

Did that really just happen?! Still pacing, I immediately call Denise for a recap.

"Hello?"

"Denise! You are not gonna believe who I'm going out with this Friday!"

"Who?"

"Adam!" I squeal, barely believing it myself. A long silence follows. I've clearly shocked her to death.

"Uh...Who?" she asks tentatively. Seriously?!!

"You know! Adam! Champagne flutes Adam."

"Ooooh. 'Mr. Park' Adam," she says. I can hear the smile in her voice. "You mean the jerk who practically yelled at you after you drove all the way to Cape Cod, then had the *nerve* to ask for a ride back?"

Oh, right. I never gave Denise the full details from the car ride. After how it ended, I figured I'd spare myself the embarrassment. I spend the next fifteen minutes filling her in and when I'm done, she's borderline hyperventilating.

"Damn, girl! I'm so proud of you."

"Proud? For what?"

"Adam asked you out and, rather than think of a million excuses, you actually said 'yes'!" This is the problem with best friends. They know you too well...and call you on your bullshit.

"Harsh, but fair. He IS super hot, though. Way hotter than even Michael." Michael was an adjunct professor at CUNY with a slight snaggletooth. He dressed like my uncle, but damn was he a god with his tongue. Denise just sucks her teeth.

"Fuck Michael. He was a two pump chump *and* he cheated on you."

Well, damn. Her voice softens a bit. She must realize she struck a nerve.

"I'm sorry, Maya. All I'm saying is that he wasn't good enough for you. You are awesome. You are funny. You are hot. And you deserve someone who's all in for you."

"Thanks, D." I've finally stopped pacing. Denise is right. Why am I overthinking this? It's just a date. It's not like it's the rest of my life. I should just focus on having fun and forget about anything else.

With D and Tiff here to help me with what to wear for my date, my apartment looks even messier than normal. Tiffany, my resident stylist, sits in the living room, using the hallway as a makeshift catwalk to judge outfits. Denise is judging too, but she's mostly here for the wine and petit fours I made for the occasion.

In the four days since Adam asked me out, he's been radio silent except to confirm our date yesterday afternoon. I used that time to stress bake macarons, chocolate eclairs, Baumkuchen, and the snack cakes we're eating tonight. If I hadn't been swamped with orders, I definitely would have gone insane.

"C'mon, Maya!" Tiffany calls from the living room. "I know you're going to look fierce in that so just come out so we can do your makeup."

I smooth my hands down my dress and take a calming breath. I do my best Tyra Banks impression when I walk down the hall and Tiffany breaks into applause.

"I knew it. Whew. Adam's not going to know what hit him!"

Denise snaps in appreciation as she brings her wine glass to sit next to Tiff.

"Damn, Tiffany! I'm going to have to use you for my dates too." Tiffany smiles at the compliment and raises her glass.

"Here's to sexy outfits and even sexier men!" We all cheers our glasses and laugh before Tiffany's face turns serious.

"So why are you so nervous about this date? Is he not that interested?"

Denise cuts in before I can answer.

"Adam is *super* interested. Maya's just got a bad case of imposter syndrome." I hand Tiffany the makeup bag while she and Denise share a look.

"Still, Maya? I would've thought you'd gotten over that." Tiffany turns to talk to Denise like I'm not in the room. I knew it was a mistake to introduce them.

"Ever since junior high, this beautiful woman has been letting assholes decide how she should feel about herself."

"Hey! I may have some baggage in that area, but I don't let them decide."

"Oh yeah?" I don't like the challenge I hear in Denise's voice. "Then prove it. Tonight, don't be 'unsure Maya'. Be 'Head Bitch In Charge Maya'."

Tiffany cheers her on as she does my mascara.

"Damn right! Let this Adam guy know he would be *lucky* to spend a night with you." My cheeks go beet red.

"*Tiffany*! It's our first real date. I doubt it will end in the bedroom."

Tiffany and Denise both look me up and down.

"It will if this dress has anything to do with it!"

Denise high fives Tiffany. What am I getting myself into?

CHAPTER THIRTEEN

Adam

At 7pm on the dot, Maya walks up to the host who gestures in my direction. We make eye contact and she gives me a small smile. Wow. She looks amazing in a burgundy dress with a plunging neckline and a flowy skirt. Her hair's up in a tight bun tonight and all I can think about is taking it down and running my fingers through it. As she approaches the table, I stand up to pull out her chair.

"You look amazing. Did you have any trouble finding parking?" She sits down across from me and it's hard not to stare at her breasts. As nice as they are, it's her shy smile that threatens to undo me.

"Thanks. And no. I actually found a spot right across the street." She lifts her menu up and holds it like a shield between us. No way. We're past that. I reach out and press her menu to the table. She bites her bottom lip and those big doe eyes look almost scared.

"Maya? Do I make you nervous?" From the way she's now clutching the strap of her purse, I already know the answer. She lets out a little puff of air, flustered.

"Well...Yes. I mean you're a customer and..." She fidgets in her seat. "I wasn't expecting you to ask me out." And here I thought I'd been coming on too strong.

"Is this not how most of your orders go?" She can tell I'm kidding by the mischievous glint in my eye. She lets out an embarrassed laugh.

"Considering the most people usually see of me is a FedEx box? Definitely not."

"Was it really a surprise, though? You had to know I was interested." I see the rosiness rising in her cheeks and her breasts. She's so cute when she's agitated.

"I knew you were flirting, but some people just flirt for fun. I didn't realize you were genuinely interested until your text." I give her a slow smile and see goosebumps rise on her arms.

"I'll be sure to be more clear next time." I take her hand and can feel her shaking. She's having trouble making eye contact too. I give her a gentle squeeze and make it my mission to help her relax.

Dinner was delicious. We got a bottle of mead for the table and shared the vegetarian hot pot. I thought Maya might not want to try it, but she said yes right away. I can't wait to see how far her adventurous streak goes. Hearing her slurp down the rice noodles and tofu put all sorts of ideas in my head.

Whether it's the mead or the great conversation, Maya's been getting more and more relaxed as the date goes on. She moved closer to me when a rowdy party was seated next to us, and her hand's been on my leg since halfway through dinner. I can barely concentrate.

Looking at the menu now, she starts to pout. I'm immediately worried.

"What's wrong, Maya?" She sighs dramatically and I feel the bottom drop out of my stomach.

"They don't have dessert here." She looks at me with a playful smile and my mouth becomes the Sahara. I am *all about* flirty Maya. I press my lips together to control a laugh.

"So you're a dessert girl, huh? Is that why you're so sweet?" The line is definitely corny, but I'm glad I risked it anyway considering the genuine laugh that erupts from her like a cheerful geyser. She gives my knee another squeeze, accidentally tickling me. I flinch away reflexively and chuckle, but she looks worried again.

"Sorry! It seems mead makes me a little handsy." I sigh and pull her hand from her lap back onto my leg.

"It's OK. You just tickled me is all." I hope it's still manly to be ticklish.

"Noted," she says with a grin, all traces of worry gone.

"So what are we going to do about dessert?" I look down at her hand and don't hesitate.

"I know a place close by that has dessert. Ice cream, butter cookies, and espresso." Her face lights up.

"You had me at ice cream. But how far is it? Can we walk from here?" This is the moment of truth.

"It's actually just two blocks from here. It's...my place?"

I don't want to scare her off, but I also don't think I can go much longer without getting Maya alone. She looks so soft and inviting and she smells so good and damn, I almost didn't make it to Friday waiting to see her.

Her eyes darken and the skin of her throat gets even more rosy. Game on. I pay quickly and lead the way out of the restaurant.

She's quiet as she walks next to me, but so am I, because it's all been leading up to this. There's no need to drown out the sounds of the city around us with small talk. We both steal looks at one another until we reach my building.

I fumble for my keys and hold the door for her before leading us to my apartment on the second floor. Once inside, she keeps walking, surveying my living room and the posters on my walls.

"So I was right about you being into indie bands," she says quietly, looking anywhere but at me. I step closer to her and nod my head.

"Guilty. But I still enjoy the classics."

She keeps looking around and I start to wonder what my apartment says about me. Does it look like I'm a player?

"I really like your place. And when I dropped you off before, I thought it was cool how close you are to so many subway lines."

I step closer.

"Is that what you were thinking?" I'm less than a foot from her, and her breath hitches when I take her hand.

"Just to be clear, Maya, I didn't bring you here to have dessert." Her eyes widen and I expect her to pull away, but she doesn't.

"I kinda figured that when you said it was at your place." I move my hands up her arms, caressing her wrists. I'm rewarded with more goosebumps. I wonder where else she's excited.

"And you're OK with that? Because if you've changed your mind, I can totally walk you to your car. No pressure." I hold my breath. Sure, there's no pressure, but there will be immense disappointment and a thirty-minute cold shower if she says she wants to leave now.

"No. I'd like to stay." I let out my breath in relief. She walks to my couch and takes a seat, one ankle crossed behind the other, ever the lady. My heart starts racing and I have to remind myself not to tackle her as I move to sit next to her.

Even though she said she wants to stay, I still feel like I need to be careful. Like one false move could send her running away again. I scoot closer to her until our knees are touching. She's watching me intently.

"So, do you do this often? Wine and dine women and then bring them to your place?" Great. My apartment must have "player" written all over it. I break eye contact.

"Actually, no. I have hookups, sure, but," I look directly into her eyes. "I don't normally bring women back to my apartment." She ponders that, and I gently place my hand on her thigh. Her skin is warm and soft and my body reacts immediately. I lean in closer, my mouth brushing her ear, and inhale deeply.

"Mmmm. You still smell so good. Is it weird that I've wanted to smell you again all night?" She shakes her head and I nuzzle my lips against her ear again. I can see her pulse racing in her throat.

She's clearly nervous, so I'm beyond surprised when she turns to face me and puts her hands on my shoulders. She trails them down to my chest before reaching for the buttons of my shirt. It turns me on how much she wants me, and I get impossibly harder in my pants.

The room is quiet except for our uneven breathing and the sounds of traffic from the street below. I leave her ear to place a kiss on her neck. It's innocent enough, until I bite down and then lick the spot.

She gasps and misses a button. I keep kissing down her throat until I reach the neckline of her dress.

"These have been driving me crazy all night," I say to her tits, before sliding my hands from her hips up her ribcage to give them a squeeze. She moans, but it sounds muffled. I look up to see her pressing her lips together. I take her face in one hand and stroke her lips with my thumb, coaxing them apart.

"There you go, baby. I wanna hear how much you like what I'm doing to you." Her mouth opens, and she's practically panting. I can't take it anymore. I have to kiss her. I lean in slowly, giving her plenty of time to retreat, before pressing my lips softly against hers.

Damn she's so sweet! Her lips are velvety and hot and I can still taste the honey from the mead on them. I tilt my head to deepen the kiss and slip my tongue into her scorching mouth.

She's completely given up trying to unbutton my shirt and instead is clinging to the fabric as I start to plunder her mouth. It's not nearly enough.

I pull away from her mouth to kiss the tops of her breasts and grab them, squeezing harder this time. She arches into my hands and I pinch the nipples I feel straining through her dress.

"Ah, Adam! Jesus!" I chuckle and pinch them again, rewarded with another moan.

"You like that, huh?" I'm kissing deeper into her cleavage now, pulling down the fabric to expose more of her to my mouth. She's clenching my shirt in fists now.

"God, yes! Adam...Shit!" She hisses out the last word, as I chose that moment to push her dress and bra down the rest of the way to take her left nipple into my mouth. Her hands abandon my shirt and move to the back of my neck, pulling my hair, pressing me harder against her. I still can't get close enough.

Frustrated, I pull the sleeves of her dress down and her bra comes with it, exposing both of her breasts to me fully. Jesus Christ. She must be a D cup at least.

"Maya," I say in awe. "You are gorgeous. I just..." I'm sure she can hear me gulp, can see my mouth practically watering from the image of her aroused and ready on my couch, her cinnamon globes heaving with every breath and tipped with what look (and taste) like dark chocolate truffles.

"I'm glad you're here," I finish, when my words finally return. She smiles at me, all signs of nervousness gone. She pushes me back against the couch and straddles my lap, wrapping her arms around my neck.

"I'm glad I'm here too." She takes my hands and places them on her hips before kissing me deeply. This kiss has been building since the drive. I spent days thinking about her, having no choice but to jerk off to her luscious curves and still waking up pitching a tent in my sheets with cum on my leg. Something about her clearly does it for me, and she's finally here, in the flesh.

The kissing gets more heated, more urgent. I move my hands down from her hips to cup her ass and start grinding her against my dick. I moan into her mouth when her movements become more explicit, matching the rhythm of my tongue in her mouth.

"Damnit, Maya. If you keep riding me like this, we're not going to make it to the main event." Her smile turns cocky, as if I've just challenged her. She widens her knees, bringing her pussy into tighter contact against my cock. I can feel the heat coming off her.

Her dress is riding up from the gyrations. I help it along, until my hands are gripping her bare ass. It feels amazing in my palms, and my dick is almost painfully hard now.

She picks up the pace of her grinding, pulling open my shirt and pressing her bare breasts against my chest—skin to skin. From the heat coming off her and the shiver when I spank her ass, I'm not the only one barreling towards release.

Except for my pants and what feels like a lace thong, we're having sex. It's startling to think how good this feels and I haven't even been inside her yet. I kiss my way down her neck to her nipples, licking and biting them as I thrust faster against her panties.

"Oh my God! I'm coming!" she screams, bucking in my lap and triggering my own orgasm. My fierce grunt is muffled by her breast and we cling tightly to each other as we unravel together.

I'm definitely in trouble.

CHAPTER FOURTEEN

Maya

After our X-rated dry humping session, Adam smacked my ass again before leaving to wash up. It's a turn-on how assertive he is in the bedroom—well, technically we're in the *living room*. It's definitely something I hope to explore further. Between the dirty talk, the nipple play, and the size of the erection I felt pushing through his pants, I knew I was a goner.

No guy has ever made me cum while still wearing my clothes. I still have on my shoes, for God's sakes! I maybe should've stopped when he warned me he was close, but making a strong, sexy man lose control is another one of my turn-ons. I tuck my completely ruined panties into my purse and hear water running in the bathroom down the hall. This seems like the perfect opportunity to snoop.

In the kitchen, he's got a decent collection of coffee, tea, and a fancy espresso machine. I see the butter cookies he mentioned in the cupboard and ice cream, vodka, and frozen peas in the freezer. True to a bachelor, the fridge contains nothing but beer and leftover pizza old enough to grow mold. Ew.

One side of his living room is a home office complete with double monitors, an ergonomic keyboard, a wireless headset and...is that a server? Note to self: ask Adam what he does that requires a home office straight out of NASA's mission control.

Now for the juicy stuff. The shelf behind his desk is full of pictures:

- Adam with an older couple–a white woman with a kind face and auburn hair and a tall, Asian man who's intimidating even in the picture.

Those must be his parents.

- Adam in a cap and gown with that couple again, plus four other men, all with the same wide smile.

Four *brothers? Wow! My parents told me it was "one and done" for them. I can't imagine a house full of that much testosterone.*

- Adam with a beautiful redhead after some sort of presentation.

- Adam with a beautiful brunette at...prom maybe?

- Adam and a beautiful blonde playing tennis.

- Adam surrounded by beautiful women at a beach

bonfire.

- Adam with–

"Someone is being nosey, I see." Adam's voice feels like an embrace and two seconds later, his hands wrap around my waist. He presses a kiss to the base of my neck and I do my best not to stiffen. I turn in his arms and paste a fake smile on my face. I need to get out of here fast.

"Busted. I got curious and started looking around." His arms loosen enough for me to move away.

"And what did you find out?" Although he lets me escape, he follows close behind, watching me.

"Nothing too bad. Your fridge is basically empty, but that's no surprise." The corners of his mouth lift, but it's not really a smile. I push onward.

"With the desk setup you have, you must do something high-tech." He nods silently. I'm almost to the door.

"And I think you have four brothers." I grab my purse from where I left it by the door.

"Anything else?" he asks, one eyebrow raised but his expression otherwise a mystery.

"No," I say, my fake smile feeling more like baring teeth.

"Then why does it feel like you're running away?" *Because I am*, I say to myself. I can't admit that seeing all those women on his shelf brought up old and deep-rooted insecurities. Insecurities I've tried to cover up with layer cake and crafting.

Insecurities that now have me worried I'm some sort of fetish for him instead of a real person.

"It's nothing like that," I scoff. I was aiming for airy, but it sounds forced to my ears. "I made the mistake of checking my email and saw that I had a really big rush order come in."

"And you have to start tonight?" His eyebrow is even higher now. I'm pretty sure he's not buying this. I bite my lip before catching myself and smile wider.

"It's just that it's a repeat client and he's kind of demanding. I want to get home and see what he's got me doing this time." He nods grimly and moves to his door, grabbing his keys.

"It's late. I'll walk you to your car." I turn to the door and reach for the locks but he gently pushes my hand out of the way. The electricity when we touch is still there, and I see him clench his jaw.

"It's no problem, really. I can—" He cuts me off with an expression that leaves no room for argument.

"I'll walk you to your car."

Safely inside my apartment, I slouch to the floor against the door. Khan runs over and makes himself at home in my lap like a bored king. Just as his deep purring starts to soothe my foul mood, a chirp from my cell phone sends him running to his perch in the living room.

Adam (Champagne Flutes)

Adam (Champagne Flutes): You make it home safe?

So let me get this right. I run out of his apartment like it's on fire and not only does he insist on walking me to my car, but now he's...checking on me? In my experience, men don't react well when you give them an epic case of blue balls. His mom must have raised him right.

Adam (Champagne Flutes)

Safe and sound. Thanks for checking.

Adam (Champagne Flutes): Good. Now you can tell me why you ran away...again.

Ugh. I'm not sure I can. I get up and kick my shoes off on the way to my bedroom.

Adam (Champagne Flutes)

Adam (Champagne Flutes): You don't think I really believe you had to run home at midnight for some special order, do you?

I dive face first into my bed fully clothed and pull the comforter all the way over my head.

Adam (Champagne Flutes)

Hmm...I guess not.

Adam (Champagne Flutes): So? What happened? One second you're in my lap, and the next you're practically clawing at the locks to get out of my apartment.

I raise an eyebrow at that. Dramatic, much?

Adam (Champagne Flutes)

Clawing at the locks? Really, Adam?

Adam (Champagne Flutes): That's what I saw. So tell me what happened.

Adam (Champagne Flutes): Did you not like what we did?

My traitorous pussy pulses in pleasure just *thinking* about what we did. From what I felt earlier, he's packing some serious heat too and I'd be lying if I said I wasn't bummed to be in my bed instead of Adam's right now.

I sigh and come out from under the covers to respond. Well, honesty *is* the best policy.

Adam (Champagne Flutes)

I loved what we did.

I can imagine Adam's frustrated sigh.

Adam (Champagne Flutes): Me too. So why are we texting now instead of picking up where we left off?

It just felt a little…intense. I've never done that before.

It was the truth…mostly. Being with him had been super intense. And amazing. Even though we didn't have sex, I can tell that, if we do,—*when* we do,—we will be fully compatible. But then I saw all those women and couldn't help but think he'd be comparing me to them if we took it any further. Plus-size clearly isn't his type, so why is he even pursuing me? My phone is silent for a few minutes.

Adam (Champagne Flutes)

Adam (Champagne Flutes): Oh. I haven't done something like that since…junior high? lol. But it definitely never felt like THAT. I really wanted to continue, if that wasn't obvious.

It was obvious. ;)

I take a deep breath, trying to summon back "Bold Maya".

Adam (Champagne Flutes)

So what would you do if I were still over there?

My phone immediately vibrates with a call. Oh shit. Of course it's Adam.

"Hello?"

"Are you sure you wanna know, Maya?" His voice sounds positively menacing. "What I would do if you were still here is definitely…*intense*. And we both know how scared you are."

I throw the covers off now. Those are fighting words.

"Scared?! I am not scared!" He laughs wickedly and I can hear him shifting his position, lying down.

"Oh yeah?" From those two words alone, I know he's about to call my bluff.

"Yeah," I say, with way less conviction now.

"So you mean to tell me that if," he pauses, clears his throat. "If instead of letting you out of my arms earlier, I would've dropped to my knees and lifted your skirt, pulling down your panties with my teeth, you still would've stayed?"

Oh. my. God! His words make my skin catch on fire, but I can't back down now.

"The joke's on you, because I took my panties off as soon as you went to the bathroom." *Take that!*

I hear Adam breathing hard, like I've just punched him in the stomach.

"That's not very nice, Maya." The words are virtually a growl. "You know I wouldn't have let you leave if I'd known." I laugh because, fetish or not, I know he's as hard as a basketweave stitch thinking about me right now.

"And what would be my punishment if you'd known that I was completely bare and wet for you?" I might be nervous in person, but my phone game is on point. I know I've caught him off guard because I hear him sit up.

"First, I would spank that beautiful ass of yours for being so naughty." I giggle mischievously.

"You seem to have a thing for my ass, Adam."

"You got that right, Maya." Again, I'm struck by how sure of himself he is. "Then, I would push you against the wall and slip my fingers inside you to see just how wet for me you are."

Damn! I guess I shouldn't be surprised he has a way with words after our previous conversations.

"Oh, I'm extremely wet," I admit, letting my fingers trail down to explore my womanhood. "From what I saw on our little car trip, your fingers are long, but they're nothing compared to what I felt sitting in your lap." I hear his breathing become more labored.

"Oh, so you were watching me?" Only a blind person wouldn't.

"Of course I was watching you. You're not the only one who can stare at someone." His breath catches. I'm enjoying shocking him with my boldness.

"Can you blame me? I mean, look at you. Whenever I'm around you, it's a struggle to maintain eye contact instead of staring at your body the whole time." I'm blushing so hard now, he can probably hear it through the phone.

"If you were here," he continues, "I would caress all of that smooth, brown skin of yours before nudging your legs wide and kissing your dripping flower, my fingers rubbing that sweet bud at the top of your mound until you came apart on my tongue." My fingers are stroking my clit now. He likely can hear me breathing heavily, but I can hear something too. Something...rhythmic.

"Adam...are you...touching yourself right now?" He laughs roughly into the receiver.

"I can't help it. I get excited just thinking about you." My head spins thinking that I have the power to make such a beautiful man weak.

"Don't tell me I'm the only one." He says this with such smugness, I'm tempted to lie, but I can't bring myself to do it.

"No," I answer shyly. "You're not the only one."

He groans like my admission hurts him.

"Fuck, Maya." His tone is admonishing. "Where is your hand right now?" I bite my lip, almost too embarrassed to respond.

"It's...in between my legs," I say hesitantly, apparently bold enough to masturbate with Adam on the phone, but not bold enough to say "pussy" aloud. He sighs.

"You're making me crazy, Maya." His voice is strained. "Are you sure you don't want me to show you how good this could be in person?"

"Don't underestimate the power of a great phone call," I counter in my best sex kitten voice.

"If I were there," I say, returning to the phone sex already in progress, "I would return the favor, unbuttoning your jeans to pull out your long, thick cock. It's already so hard for me." The rhythmic sounds resume, and I match my own fingers to the pace.

"I would swirl my tongue around your tip before swallowing as much of you as I could fit in my mouth. I would press my nails into your thighs while bobbing up and down on your dick, mixing agony and ecstasy, teasing you until you begged me to let you cum." Faster rhythmic sounds. I shove my panties down to my knees for unfettered access.

"And when you finally did, I would take you up to the hilt, feeling your hot load as it flowed down my eager throat."

"Uh, uh, fuck!!" I love how vocal Adam is. His moans and sighs make me hot and I feel my orgasm crash over me shortly after.

"Ahh! Goodness!"

The phone is forgotten next to me on my bed as I drift, weightless following my release. Maybe minutes later, I bring it to my ear in time to hear Adam regaining his composure on the other end.

"Maya? You still there?"

"Yes," I reply, still out of breath.

"That was incredible." He sounds dreamy. I'm floating somewhere past Venus myself. "When are you going to let me get inside of you for real?" Adam actually sounds like he's pouting. I try to keep the grin out of my voice.

"I don't know. That felt pretty real to me."

"You know what I mean, Maya." Yes, I do.

"Well, how 'bout we just keep seeing each other, and take it from there." If I'm just a phase, he'll get tired of me before I can get hurt.

"OK," he says, doubt in his voice. "I'll text you."

"I'll be here."

CHAPTER FIFTEEN

Adam

"For the third time, guys, this is no contact!" Damon yells from the ground. I knew inviting my brothers out for flag football would be entertaining and they have not let me down. I laugh when I see Cory trying to do a sleeper hold before Damon pushes him off. After all that, Damon's flag remains attached to his waistband.

"Seriously, guys," Damon says through a frown. "If I get injured, my whole season will be at risk. Plus, my coach'll kill me." He brushes the grass off his clothes and gingerly tests the range of motion on his arm.

"Sorry, bro," Cory yells, running to join everyone on the sideline. "When that adrenaline kicks in, I can't help myself." We all roll our eyes, because there doesn't seem to be *any* time when Cory isn't competitive. He once fractured his ankle racing Damon through a club parking lot after one too many Long

Island iced teas. He's mostly harmless, though. I throw Damon a water bottle from the cooler and chugs his Gatorade. He stands up, gym bag in hand.

"I'm gonna have to call it, guys. I can't come into court tomorrow with a sprained ankle or bruised ribs because one of you went turbo." Henry looks meaningfully at Cory, who suddenly finds the grass stains on his shirt fascinating. Noah nods in agreement.

"Yeah. Let's call it a tie." As usual, the twins are on the same page.

"Wusses," I hear Cory mumble under his breath.

"C'mon, Cory. Cut them some slack. They are almost senior citizens!" For that comment, I get a glare and a towel to the face from both Noah and Henry, but Henry can't hide his smile.

"So what are everyone's plans for the rest of the day?" Noah asks. He grabs a water before helping me pack the flags. "I'm taking three of the five New Kids on the Block out to dinner before their show at the Garden tonight."

"New Kids on the Block at the Garden?" Cory scoffs. "Those guys haven't been cool since I was in elementary school."

"Revival tours are trending, bro. The show has been sold out for weeks." I detect a note of pride in Noah's voice. Landing NKOTB was a major reason he made partner two years ago.

"Nothing exciting for me, I'm afraid. I've got to walk my client through a settlement offer on Monday, so I'll be studying tonight," Henry says. All of us groan in response and he rolls his eyes.

"Well," Cory puffs out his chest with pride, "I have a hot date tonight with the girl one floor below me. She came up to complain about the noise last time I had company over and I asked her out." He wiggles his eyebrows for emphasis on the word "company" and I grin.

"Leave it to you to get a date out of a noise complaint," I laugh. Though none of us have girlfriends, Cory might be the biggest player I know.

"What about you, baby bro?" Noah asks as we all start walking towards the subway.

"Nah. No hot date for me." We keep walking and I wonder if I should tell them. Why not? They might even be happy for me.

"I *have* started seeing someone," I admit. All four of my brothers stop in their tracks and exchange looks. No one says anything. Cory's jaw actually drops open.

"Wow. That is not the reaction I was expecting." I resume walking and Noah is the first to snap out of it, jogging to catch up.

"Our bad, Adam. This is just the first time you've mentioned getting serious with anyone." Cory still looks upset, his shoulders hunched and brow furrowed. I might be the youngest, but Cory has everyone beat in immaturity.

"Don't apologize for me. I for one am shocked the guy who used to set a timer on cuddling now has a girlfriend." I'm not surprised at Cory, but even Damon and Henry are keeping quiet. So much for our "band of brothers".

"OK, calm down, everyone. I'm not getting serious; it's only been one date. She's not my girlfriend or anything." *Not yet.* I see nothing but doubt on their faces and try my best to change the subject back to the game before everyone disperses. Henry's off to Grand Central to catch the Metro North, Noah gets an Uber, Cory opts to walk to his place on Columbus Circle, and Damon and I take the train heading to Brooklyn.

We push through the turnstiles and find the B train arriving on the track. At least the subway's on my side today. We push through a group of lost tourists (do you really need to look at the map right in front of the subway doors?) and grab a couple seats.

"So tell me about this girl you're seeing." Damon looks genuinely curious, but I've learned my lesson.

"No way, man. Fool me once; shame on you. Fool me twice, I start to look like an asshole." His eyes soften and he nudges me with his knee.

"No really, baby bro. You just caught us off guard. I wanna know about the woman who made Adam Park change his wicked ways." I want to know more about Maya too. I lean back and resign myself to being the butt of a few jokes.

"Well...Her name is Maya," I start slowly. Damon nods for me to continue. "She did the favors for Bryan's engagement party and then gave me a ride back from the Cape." Damon sits up straighter in his seat.

"I thought you rode with Emily."

"That was the plan, but she actually came onto me pretty strong at the end of the party. I figured four hours alone in the car with her after turning her down yet again would be pretty awkward." Though I haven't told Bryan about his sister, all of my brothers know. He simply nods and grabs an energy bar from his bag.

"So what does Maya look like? Is she cute?" What a ridiculous question.

"Of course she's cute," I say with only the tiniest hint of defensiveness in my voice. Damon looks at me expectantly when I don't elaborate.

"Well...?" Damon is clearly waiting for a full description complete with height and bra size. I roll my eyes.

"I don't have a picture of her or anything. She's cute. Dark hair, dark eyes, seriously curvy, and she wears her hair in locs." Damon chews slowly and is silent for a while.

"So...she's Black?"

"Yes," I say with warning in my voice. He holds up his hands.

"No offense, bro. I'm just trying to get a picture. And she's curvy? That's new for you." Although his words are rubbing me wrong, he is right. Whether intentional or not, I've never gone for bigger girls in the past. But Maya is different. I was drawn to her right away, curves and all. He would be too if he saw her. That thought alone makes me want to sock him in the jaw.

"I admit she's not my usual type, but she's mad cool. She's funny, she's smart, and for those reasons, I plan to keep her as far away from you guys as possible." I punch his arm playfully and he rolls his eyes.

"Whatever. You know you'll have to bring her to meet Mom and Dad if it gets serious, right?"

I pretend interest in my phone and Damon smirks before finishing his energy bar in one bite. None of us have ever brought a girl home to the family. Who knows how that would go or if they would accept Maya. But I'm getting way ahead of myself! We need to go on quite a few more dates before I have to worry about that.

Damon gets off two stops later and I spend the rest of my ride thinking about what he said. I caught her looking at my pictures, pictures that all feature a certain physical type. Could that be why she ran away the other night?

CHAPTER SIXTEEN

Maya

Denise hasn't said anything for a solid minute; that's a record for her. I sip my gin & tonic and look around the bar. Ever since they switched DJs, the vibe here hasn't been the same. It went from Mos Def and Jill Scott to Lorde and Doja Cat. Plus, they switched to these tiny bar stools and my left butt cheek feels like it's hanging on for dear life.

"So…" Denise is still wrapping her head around what I told her about my date with Adam. "You made him cum in his pants, drove home, and then proceeded to have phone sex?" The bartender quirks an eyebrow. Clearly she overheard us. Luckily it's too dark in here for anyone to see me blushing.

"Could you *not* share my business with the whole bar, D?" I look around to see if anyone else is eavesdropping on our conversation.

"That just sounds like a lot of work to me. Didn't you want to sleep with him? I'm talking in real life, not over the phone." *Boy, had I!* I want to go over to his place right now. I take another sip of my drink so she can't see the horniness on my face.

"Of course I did, but I told you what happened. I just didn't want to become some kind of big girl experiment." Especially not when I could see myself developing real feelings for Adam. D looks doubtful.

"So you saw a few pics of skinny women," she says sternly. "So what! You don't know that he slept with all of them." She starts counting off on her fingers. "They could be *friends*, *teammates*, whatever! A pic doesn't guarantee they're an ex."

I pause half an inch above my straw. Huh. Why *did* I assume those were all ex girlfriends?

"Hmmm." Denise takes that as a sign to keep making her case.

"Not only that, but even if those *were* all exes, didn't *he* ask *you* out even after you freaked and drove off that first night? Didn't *he* call *you* back and initiate phone sex after you ran away?"

"I initiated the phone sex," I argue weakly. She smirks at me.

"Potato, *potahto*. This guy definitely seems interested in *you*, not some skinny chicks." I have to admit she's making a lot of sense. She knows it too, based on the righteous look in her eyes as she sips her cosmo.

"OK," I admit begrudgingly. "I see your point. I told him we should just keep seeing each other and see how things go."

"That was a smart move, Maya." *I'm glad you approve, professor.* I try not to roll my eyes. "Don't overthink this. He's a hottie who wants to spend some time with you. You want to spend some time with him, too. End of story." Gosh, I wish I could see things this clearly on my own. Alone, my mind's default setting seems to be "worst case scenario". Denise swirls her drink with a straw thoughtfully.

"We are skipping over one very big detail."

"What?"

"You were going to fuck him on the *first date*? Go, Maya! I didn't know you had it in you." She cheers and pats me on the back while the two young guys sitting next to us chuckle under their breath. I duck my head and wish for the cloak of invisibility.

"Denise! Oh my God. You're going to get us kicked out of here." She smirks while flagging down the bartender.

"For talking about sex in a bar? I think not. So, spill. How did you go from needing your girls' help to get ready to almost doing the horizontal tango on the first night?" She wiggles her eyebrows suggestively and I can't help but giggle.

"Well, he's just very..." *What is the word?* "Alluring? Maybe 'irresistible' is a better word. He kept whispering in my ear close enough for me to feel his lips and touching my hands and looking at me." I sigh like a lovestruck schoolgirl. "Before I knew it, I was the one touching HIM and asking about 'dessert'." Denise looks impressed.

"It sounds like Mr. Park has game. Do you have a picture? I need to see who got you so worked up you forgot you're basically a prude." I roll my eyes at that. She thinks I'm a prude because I normally have a three-date rule, while she barely has a three-hour rule. It may work for her, but it's not my style.

"How would I have a picture? Was I supposed to sneak a pic while I was driving?"

"How about his social media?" I stare at her blankly and D clutches imaginary pearls.

"You *still* haven't stalked his social media yet? We must remedy this right away." She takes out her phone and starts typing faster than a hacker in "The Matrix".

"Bingo!" she says, after less than a minute. She definitely has skills. I lean over to peek at her phone.

"Adam Park...Born in Brooklyn, lives in Brooklyn...Stanford alum. Is this your guy?" I nod when I see charcoal locks and midnight eyes staring back at me. *Don't tell me I'm affected by just a profile picture now*...I sit back to drink my watered down cocktail while Denise browses his pictures.

"Oh wow. No wonder you almost jumped his bones!" Denise fans herself and I grab the phone from her hand. I'm not a big fan of social media stalking, but she started it. What I see makes my throat go dry and my kitty immediately starts purring.

Almost all of Adam's pics are blatant thirst traps:

- Adam shirtless doing squats in the gym

- Adam jogging along the boardwalk in gray sweatpants

(swoon!)

- Adam shirtless showing off his muscles in the mirror

- Adam shirtless looking like he's naked (!) in bed

D has joined me in drooling over his pics, her chin resting on my shoulder.

"That boy is *fine*. And he's into Black women, huh?" I push her off my shoulder and glare at her teasingly.

"Back off, D. He's mine." *Or he* will *be*. She laughs and finishes the last of her cosmo. I excuse myself to the bathroom and make my way through the crowd.

Away from the din of some Drake or SZA song, I pull out my cell. There's no time like the present to take control of the situation. The liquid courage flowing through my veins certainly doesn't hurt.

Adam

Hey, Adam. I had fun the other day.

He responds immediately.

Adam

Adam: Me too. So when can we do it again?

I smile like the who ate the canary. Thank God he's as eager as I am.

Adam

Phone sex?

Adam: lol. No, a date. Preferably ending at my place. Or yours.

Are you free Wednesday?

Adam: Nah. I have a work thing. What about Friday?

I'm going to DC for my parent's wedding anniversary.

Adam: Ah, bummer.

Really, Adam? LOL

Adam: I mean, not bummer about the anniversary, lol. You know what I mean.

Adam: Are you ever free during the day?

Yeah. I set my own hours. That's one of the perks of being a small business owner.

Adam: Sweet. If you're willing to tag along with me to help register for some wedding gifts, we can grab lunch after.

Sounds good. Text me the details. Gotta get back to my friend.

There. I return to the bar and Denise and I celebrate my upcoming date and newfound confidence with shots. Adam is too hot and the attraction between us is too strong to ignore. Fetish, phase, or otherwise, I'm not letting this opportunity slip through my fingers.

CHAPTER SEVENTEEN

Adam

An instrumental version of Smokey Robinson's "Cruisin'" comes through the ceiling speakers. In the mostly-empty department store, we pass a display of mannequins enjoying beach day in the Hamptons before reaching the Home section. Salespeople hover just one rack over, ready to pounce.

Peaking through dishware at Maya, I realize now that my lunch date plan was fatally flawed. How am I supposed to get her alone again when we're miles from my apartment, in the middle of the day, and I have to be back at my office for a 3:30 PM meeting? Registering for wedding gifts hardly yields the same opportunities for seduction and innuendo as late night dinner and dancing, but I couldn't wait to see her again.

Even under the harsh fluorescents, her skin looks like the most decadent milk chocolate and my mouth waters at the thought of letting her melt on my tongue. The honey undertones of her skin are accentuated by a teal skirt and white peasant blouse. Today, she wears her hair in a pattern wrap with gold hoop earrings that make her look like Nefertiti. Her neck is long and slender, begging to be touched. She looks so utterly feminine that I have to control my urge to knock her over the head and drag her to my cave to have my way with her. Instead, I'm stuck wandering around a department store with a scanner looking for candelabras and mixers.

She surprised the shit out of me when she texted me after playing it so cool the other night. I could've sworn she was blowing me off with the "lets just see where this goes" bullshit. That's usually *my* line, and I really wasn't digging the role reversal.

It was a pleasant surprise, though, seeing as how she's responsible for one of the best orgasms of my life and we haven't even had sex yet. She's going out of town this weekend too. Damn. *How does she have me jonesing this bad already?* I think to myself. Then our eyes meet, my mouth goes dry, and it makes total sense.

"Adam?! Adam, is that you?" Oh shit. Not now! Making her way toward me is Candy. She's a curvaceous redhead and a former member of my roster until a few months ago when she tried to spend the night. As usual, she's decked out head to toe in lululemon to show off a body she earned teaching Zumba six days a week.

Because my karma is for shit, Maya sees Candy the same time I do and turns to watch the whole scene unfold, eyebrow raised. This is not going to go well for me.

"Candy, hi!" I say through practically clenched teeth. Maya presses her lips together to suppress a smile and pretends to be engrossed in the napkin rings. She's still within earshot, though. Candy goes in for a hug and I step back to give her a handshake instead. Both her and Maya notice.

"I tried to call you a few times but it kept going to voicemail." I clear my throat and look anywhere but at her. "Are you avoiding me?" She's using a pouty, baby voice which used to sound cute but now sounds like nails on a chalkboard. I guess we didn't do enough talking for it to bother me before.

"No. I've just really busy with work." I want to end the conversation as soon as possible, but I don't want to be a dick. I doubt that would go over well with Maya watching. "How are you? How have you been?" Hopefully we'll wrap up the small talk and she'll be on her way. I take a step towards Maya, who's been doing her best to hide behind the espresso machines.

"As you can see, I'm still teaching." Candy twirls around so I can see her body fully. Christ, this is awkward. "Equinox even gave me another class on Thursdays."

"That's awesome," I say, moving even closer to Maya. I take her hand and intertwine our fingers. Luckily, Candy doesn't notice Maya's split second flinch at the unexpected contact. "Maya and I are here helping a friend get registered."

Candy turns to see Maya for the first time. I can see the wheels turning behind her eyes, trying to figure out who Maya is to me. *Me too, Candy.* She pastes a bright smile on her face and extends her manicured hand. Maya shakes it politely.

"Great to meet you, Maya. How do you know Adam here?"

I look at Maya with pleading eyes, hoping she sees fit to spare me from further humiliation. Hers are mischievous and I hold my breath.

"We actually met...online...a few weeks ago," she says, her eyes still smiling. My heart resumes beating at her willingness to play along, and I see Candy's smile fray around the edges.

"Wow. A few weeks." Candy looks a bit dazed. "And now you're on a date...during the *day*?" Fucking great. Maya must think I'm "Mr. Booty Call" now. Which...I suppose...was true with *Candy...and a lot of other women.* But things are different with Maya.

Maya looks at Candy with sympathy and her hand loosens in my grip. Shit.

"I wouldn't say—"

"I'm sorry, Candy," I interrupt, squeezing Maya's hand tighter. A sinking feeling in the pit of my stomach says she was about to say *I wouldn't say it's a date*, and it's time for a Hail Mary. Both women look at me expectantly.

"I wasn't always a gentleman when we...used to hang out." Candy's smile is completely gone now, probably because I referred to six months of late night hook ups as "hanging out". But it feels like the truth is way overdue. The expression on Maya's face is unreadable, but she hasn't pulled her hand away.

"But now you are? Two months since we last spoke and *now* you're ready to date?"

"I..." What am I supposed to say? I can't admit that time had nothing to do with it. That a date never occurred to me before...Well, before Maya. "I'm sorry."

Candy lets out a tired sigh before pushing the corners of her mouth up and turning to Maya.

"It was great to meet you, Maya. If you're ever in the area, I teach classes at the Columbus Circle Equinox on Mondays, Wednesdays, and Fridays. The other days, I'm at the Bryant Park location."

"It was nice to meet you too, Candy."

Candy practically jogs away from us. Maya turns to me with an eyebrow raised.

"Seems like there's a story there." I grab her price scanner and walk us toward the check-out desk.

"I think we're done here. I'll give you all the gory details over lunch.

Maya's eyes flutter closed briefly after she swallows a small bite of shrimp linguini. She actually lets out a little hum of appreciation. Once again, spending time with Maya has me wishing

I could be her next meal. Her sensual reactions to everything (from pasta to a tweak of her nipples) are a huge turn-on. I munch on my chicken caesar salad, watching her closely.

"So you're one of *those* guys, huh? That give the 'not looking for anything serious' speech?" I freeze, my fork halfway to my mouth. Although she's teasing, I can see judgment in her eyes too.

I dared to hope we could leave the Candy drama back at Macy's when I made it through the appetizer unscathed. No such luck. I put down my fork and give a small shrug, feeling almost...*ashamed*(?) of my ability to get almost any woman in bed. That's a first.

"I used to be, I guess."

"Oh yeah? When did you stop? Candy's been trying to reach out." She playfully swats my hand before taking a sip of her club soda. The suction of her full lips around the straw has me imagining something else and I adjust in my seat.

"June 28th," I say quietly. Judging by her stunned silence, she remembers that's the day we met. I look into her eyes meaningfully until we're interrupted by the waiter. We order (gin & tonic for me and another club soda for her) and she breaks the tension by checking her phone.

"You're making me feel like quite the lush over here." She smiles warmly and puts down her phone.

"Sorry. I have to finish up some monogramed blankets for a corporate event and my needle work comes out crooked whenever I try to do it tipsy." I burst out laughing, covering my mouth with my napkin to keep from spitting my drink on her.

"*Whenever you try to do it tipsy*? That sounds like you've tried to do it quite a few times." She smiles bashfully and takes another bite of her lunch.

"I guess that's another perk of being a small business owner. You don't have to wait until after hours to have a drink."

"Unless you're doing monograms," I correct. She giggles softly and tucks in a loose loc that fell from her head wrap. I put my fork down and look at her directly.

"So...Are you finally going to tell me the real reason you left the other night?" She's obviously startled. She must've thought I would let it drop after the phone sex. Nope.

"I told you," she stammers. "It was just intense." I consider this for a moment.

"It *was* intense. Intense and extremely hot." Her skin is flushed and she takes a sip of water. "Tell me it wasn't just me who wanted to continue...in person." She looks away shyly and shakes her head.

"No. I wanted to stay." I let out a breath I didn't know I was holding.

"Then why did you ask to leave when I came back out? Be honest. I can tell you're not telling me something." Her shoulders go rigid; she's clearly feeling defensive.

"We just met. How can you tell that?" *Because I've felt strangely close to you ever since we met.* I shrug again.

"I don't know. It's just a feeling...Am I wrong?" I take her hand in mine and feel her shiver.

"No. You're not wrong." I love that she doesn't bother trying to lie. Something tells me I would know if she did.

"So?" She's silent for so long, I think she might not answer. I keep stroking her hand and she finally sighs.

"I was looking around your place. I know I shouldn't have but..." She takes a deep breath and looks up to meet my eyes. "Looking at your pictures...and even today, meeting Candy...you definitely have a *type*. A type that looks nothing like me." She looks down again. "If I'm being honest, it kinda threw me off."

The waiter senses our uneasiness and quickly serves our drinks before retreating. I reach out to lift Maya's chin until we're eye to eye.

"Look. I admit a lot of the women I've hung out with have looked similar." I swallow before continuing. "It was just...easier that way. They didn't want anything serious and neither did I." Maya tries to pull her hand away but I hold on tighter.

"I obviously don't feel like that with you." I'm relieved to see a small smile forming on her beautiful lips.

"So you want something *serious* with me, huh?" It's my turn to blush now. I nervously clear my throat and start digging into my food. She giggles lightly and thankfully lets the subject drop.

CHAPTER EIGHTEEN

Maya

Mom and Dad are positively glowing with happiness. Rather than a banquet hall, they chose their backyard for an elegant anniversary soiree, complete with white twinkle lights, orchid flower arrangements, and a live band playing love songs from Al Green and Stevie Wonder. They descended the steps of their deck like royalty, and the new pastor at Union Temple Baptist Church helped them renew their vows for another forty years.

I spent my first night back home judging potential anniversary party outfits; Mom ultimately went with a dove gray, full length gown with a bead and lace bodice. Like me, her locs reach past her waist, though her crown has been almost fully gray for decades. She looks stunning, like Angela Basset in "Black Panther".

My father, on the other hand, looks a little like Arnold Schwarzenegger if he were 6'3" and as dark-skinned as Wesley Snipes. His Caesar cut has started showing salt and pepper on the temples and he has an impressive beard. He looks particularly dashing next to my mother in a henley collar shirt and a bronze metallic suit.

Leaning against the open bar watching them slow dance, I look at my romantic role models in awe, trying not to sulk that I haven't found a love like theirs. Then another text comes in.

Adam

Adam: You can't tell me you're wearing thigh highs when you're 200 miles away. :(

Oops. Was that me being a tease again? ;)

Adam: Naughty, naughty. Maya.

Adam: I'm starting to think you WANT me to spank you. ;)

My cheeks immediately redden and I can't stop the smile forming on my face. As the band takes a break and I formulate a steamy response, Mom joins me at the bar. I quickly shove my phone in my clutch.

"Two champagnes, please."

She's out of breath from dancing and a light sheen of sweat covers her forehead. How does she even look regal sweaty?!

She leans back, facing the dance floor, and nudges me with her elbow.

"So when are you going to tell me about the boy who's had you worked up all weekend?" She's looking pointedly at my purse with the "mom" twinkle in her eye that says there's no point in denying it. Still, I've always been hesitant to discuss men with my parents. As soon as they hear the word "boyfriend", they start browsing wedding venues and dropping hints about grandchildren.

"I don't know what you're talking about, Mom," I say, with what I hope sounds like indifference. Time to change the subject. "The ceremony really is beautiful. You did a fantastic job."

She looks like she might not take the flattery bait, but her eyes soften as she surveys the party.

"Thanks, honey. It's a shame you won't get to join us in church tomorrow. The pastor is making a special anniversary announcement during service." I do my best not to roll my eyes. I might be able to avoid telling my mom about Adam, but a trip home isn't complete without a serving of guilt.

"I know. I'm sorry, Mom. Something came up at work and I have to get back early." Mom raises an eyebrow and looks at Dad mingling with friends and family.

"Hmmm. I thought you left Sharp, Smith & Haley so you could set your own hours, not miss your parents' 40th anniversary." *Nice, Mom.* I down my lemon drop and signal the bartender for another.

"I didn't miss it, Mom. As you may have noticed, I'm standing right here, right now, at your party." Mom's look of warning lets me know I've gotten too sassy for her liking.

"Sorry, Mom. It's just a new client with a big order. I thought you'd be happy my business is growing." From the look on her face, my mild passive aggressiveness has paid off. Mom was furious I left a stable job in finance, even if it was just as an executive assistant for the Investor Relations department. Never mind that I only took the job at SSH for the paycheck when I didn't land an art internship after graduation. Even when I worked there, I was always creating.

Luckily my 9 to 5 earned me enough seed money to give notice three years ago. After some prickly years between us, even Mom had to admit It's Personal was more than just a hobby. Hell, I payed off my college loans and my rent a year in advance! Dad remained the conscientious objector as he always did when the women in his life were fighting.

"I am happy about your work, Maya. And I'm overjoyed you're here. I just wish we had you for more than one night." I smile and give her a big hug.

"I know, Mom. And I promise I'll make it up to you by coming out next month for mani-pedis or something." She smiles and gives me a peck on the cheek before grabbing the flutes.

"It's a date. Have a safe trip back, baby girl. I have to save your father from another one of Sam's get rich quick pitches." The "Sam" in question works at the neighborhood market. Ten years ago, Dad made the mistake of making small talk. Sam's been talking Dad's ear off ever since, though they've become real friends in the process. Dad even joined Sam's fantasy football league.

I gulp down the last of my cocktail and head for the side gate. I can't risk going through the house where I might run into someone; I've got a train to catch.

The hot water washes over me and I feel the tension from the train ride swirl down the drain. I am *so* glad I decided to catch the Amtrak home tonight. Mom and Dad looked amazing and forty years is definitely worth celebrating, but one night on the pullout couch in the living room is more than enough. That and I've been so anxious to see Adam all day, I'm practically sweating.

Last night, we had phone sex so erotic, my climax would have woken up my parents if I hadn't grabbed a throw pillow to cover my mouth in time. Then all day today he sent me sweet and sexy texts that made me want to climb the walls. I had no choice but to tell my mom I had to leave right after the party. I felt bad for lying, but her sly smiles every time I left to answer a text made it seem like she may have guessed the real reason I was leaving early.

I dry off and use my favorite vanilla sandalwood body butter. I rub the cream all over my thighs, breasts, stomach; anywhere I think Adam might touch. I dab pink pepper perfume on all my pulse points and the top of my mound. He's commented on my smell before and I want to be irresistible tonight.

I choose a black lace thong and a strapless black and purple lace bra before shimmying into an off-the-shoulder, black, bodycon dress with plenty of ruching to accentuate my assets. Finally, I slip on a pair of black stilettos. I can't wear them for more than an hour, but I don't plan to. I look in the mirror and see a pinup vixen staring back at me. If my flirty texts back didn't get him worked up, this outfit definitely will.

On the way to Adam's apartment, I listen to Floetry, Sade, Jill Scott, and Maxwell. The music sets a sensual mood and strengthens my resolve. Though I'm still a bit nervous, I'm positive tonight will *not* end on the phone.

I find a spot right in front of his place and receive a few whistles from passersby that confirm I look as hot as I feel. Adam answers the intercom moments after I buzz him, sounding a bit drowsy. This ought to wake him up.

"Hello?"

"Hey," I say, doing my best Kathleen Turner impression. "It's me."

He buzzes me in with lightning speed and opens the door just as I reach the top of the stairs. He's barefoot and wearing nothing but jeans and a lopsided smirk. The heat in his eyes sets me on fire.

"Maya." He smiles roguishly as he looks me over from head to toe. "I thought you were out of town." From the look on his face, the arrogant bastard knew exactly what he was doing to me all night and day. I had no choice but to come.

He steps aside to let me in. As soon as the door is closed, he grabs me and kisses me like something out of "From Here to Eternity". His hands are everywhere, feeling my ass, my hips, my waist, nearly ripping the fabric covering my breasts. He pushes inside to feel my stiff peaks and moans roughly against my mouth. He leans his forehead against mine, still breathing heavily.

"I'm sorry," he murmurs, "but you knew what you were doing with that dress." I'm gasping from the kiss, my hands resting lightly on his chest. I can feel the goosebumps on his smooth skin.

"I brought wine," I say, still leaning against his forehead. He intertwines his fingers with mine and pulls me in the direction of what I assume is his bedroom.

"Later," he growls.

CHAPTER NINETEEN

Adam

I knew I wasn't playing fair calling and texting Maya those naughty things, but not being able to touch her was driving me crazy. I imagined her aroused, growing more and more desperate with each text, and I couldn't help but push her over the edge.

And now I have her alone in my room. Her lips are puffy from my kisses, her tits are heaving with each breath, and she's stepping out of those heels and slinking towards me like she wants to eat me alive. I jerked off twice today already and still my dick is hard as calculus, pushing painfully against the zipper of my jeans at the sight of her.

She starts to pull down the sleeves of her dress and I put my hand on hers to stop the movement. Her eyes hold an unspoken question.

"Let *me* undress you," I whisper. My hands are shaking as I sit on the bed and position her hips in front of me. I touch the skin of her inner thighs and stroke up and down, enjoying the shudder coming over her body. I take my time, each stroke coming closer to the lace of her panties. When I graze my thumb over her engorged bud, her knees buckle slightly and she grabs my shoulders to right herself.

I stay on her clit, rubbing back and forth through the lace. I feel her wetness soaking through and her hips unconsciously move with the rhythm of my hand. Without warning, I push aside her panties and plunge into her aching sex, never letting up on the pressure against her clit. She's moaning now, and her legs are trembling with the beginning of an orgasm.

She's so responsive to my touch that my mouth is watering, eager to taste her. I withdraw from her to pull her panties down and she whimpers.

"Don't worry, baby. I won't leave you hanging." I push her dress up, exposing her glistening curls to me. God, she's beautiful. I kneel down to get a better angle and lean in to taste the first drops of her nectar on my tongue. When I start to french kiss her pussy just as passionately as I did her mouth, her body jerks almost violently. I wrap one arm around her hips to steady her while using the other to push two fingers in her, stroking in and out as if it were my cock. She's so hot and slippery and I can tell from the involuntary shaking of her hips that she's close.

"God, Adam. Oh my God!" I suck harder on her clit and stroke faster until she explodes in my mouth, her pussy clenching my fingers so hard I'm disappointed my dick wasn't inside her.

I waste no time standing up and pulling her dress over her head. She's wobbling slightly from the afterglow of the orgasm and I feel like beating my chest in triumph. For taking the train back early, I'm going to make her cum at least twice more. She's got nothing on but a strapless bra; her dress is bunched uselessly around her waist, covering absolutely nothing. I kiss and lick her neck as I reach behind her back to undo the clasp and push her dress down until it lies crumpled on the floor. Now she stands completely nude in front of me.

"Christ, Maya. How could you ever think I wasn't interested in you with a body like this?" Even after cumming in my mouth, my comment makes her blush. How can she be so sweet and so seductive at the same time? I kick off my jeans and boxers so fast I nearly rip them and start to pull her down on the bed, but she resists. Before I get deja vu from our first date, she trails her fingers down my chest and wraps her warm hands around my cock. I thrust against her, the feeling too overwhelming to stay still.

"'Don't worry, baby. I won't leave you hanging.'" Her smile is mischievous as she echoes my words and she leans forward to nip my earlobe with her teeth. I feel a bead of precum leave the head of my dick and she spreads it over my slit with the pad of her thumb. *Fuck!* "I told you I always return the favor."

She positions her knees on the floor between my feet and places a kiss on my left thigh before licking all the way up to the base of my dick. The hiss I let out might as well be the sound of my soul leaving my body. My balls draw tighter in preparation.

She drags her nails up and down my thighs in contrast to the licks from her scorching mouth and it feels so amazing I moan out loud. I look down and can't help but see her gorgeous breasts hanging beneath me; her nipples are like diamonds when I reach down to cup them. *Goddamn*! As hard as I am, I might poke her eye out.

She finally stops the exquisite torture of her nails to cup my balls with one hand and firmly grasp my dick with the other. She licks her lips before swallowing just the tip of my dick. I buck off the bed, inadvertently pushing another two inches into her mouth.

She laughs around my dick, creating a thrilling vibration that thickens me further against her tongue. I reach for her head to pull her off before I bust in her mouth prematurely.

"Maya...uh...Fuck. Maya, baby, wait." She takes me all the way in and I can feel her tonsils against the head of my cock. I grit my teeth against the intense pleasure. "God, this feels incredible but...mmm...please don't make me cum yet."

After last time, I know she might not stop, even if I warn her, but this time she begrudgingly releases me with a pop and sits back on her feet. From the look on her face, I can tell she's proud of her work. One more lick and I would've lost it.

I pull her onto the bed beside me and reach for the drawer of my bedside table. Before I can open it, she snatches the condom out of my hand and rolls it on my dick, forcing another hiss from my lips with the contact. She pushes me onto my back and straddles my lap before enveloping me one excruciating inch at a time. We both groan in pleasure when I'm fully seated inside her.

I grab hold of her hips and never break eye contact as she begins to move, pulling me in and out of her tight channel with delicious friction. My orgasm builds at a furious pace and I reach out and rub her clit to bring her along for the ride.

Seconds later, she tightens around me like a vice, crying out and arching against me. The feeling is too good, too real, and I spill inside her, holding her hips so tightly I know I'll leave a mark. She slumps down onto my chest, her breath fanning my neck.

"Amazing" is too mundane a word for how great that was. "Marvelous" and "extraordinary" come close. That was unbelievable. The connection between us is undeniable. I pull her tighter against me and whisper in her ear.

"You're fucking mine, Maya. No one else's. MINE."

If me being honest freaks her out, she's lying to herself about what is clearly happening between us. This is something special. No more running away.

CHAPTER TWENTY

Maya

Adam's declaration rings true in my ears, leaving little room for debate. I absolutely want him,—so strongly I feel desire in my fingernails and even the ends of my hair—but I have to at least negotiate the terms. Too many men in the past have demanded loyalty while offering none in return.

"And you're mine too, Adam. Possession goes both ways." I settle even further onto his softening dick and look him directly in the eyes. He nods. I rise up off his lap and he grabs my hand before I can reach for the blanket at the end of his bed. In our eagerness to make love, it's still made.

Ugh! *Make love*? It's such a flowery phrase. I feel something powerful for Adam, but I think it's too soon for the L word, even in this context. But *Fuck*? That's too impersonal a word for what we did. Do you look in the eyes of someone you just fuck? Do you text someone you just fuck all day? You certainly don't demand exclusivity from someone you just fuck.

"You're not running away, are you?" His eyes silently plead with me. They are pools of passion and longing. Though it's a fair question given our last date, I bristle at the question.

"Just freshening up, and grabbing some of that wine I mentioned. Well, *tried* to mention." I give him a wink and pad softly down the hall, my pussy still squeezing with aftershocks. I try two doors before finding the bathroom, lock myself in, and brace my hands on the sink.

Damn. I'm completely naked. I should've grabbed the blanket. Or maybe my dress. There's nothing like catching your naked body under harsh fluorescent light hunched over a vanity to snap you out of the mood. I lower my eyes to keep myself from launching a fault-finding mission; I tend to take them whenever a mirror is around.

Ms. Nappy Head...Thunder thighs!...Try Jenny Craig!...Call me when you lose 50 pounds!

Stop it! I may not be an expert on guys, but I'm pretty sure insecurity is frowned upon. I splash cold water on my face and think back to India.Arie's lyrics.

"I'm not the average girl from your video
And I ain't built like a supermodel
But I learned to love myself unconditionally
Because I am a queen"

I repeat the words over and over like a mantra and feel my confidence build as I use a moist towelette to wipe myself clean.

I open the door to find Adam standing right in front of me with the wine and two glasses. He's wearing nothing but a grin on his face. I reflexively drop my eyes to the floor and he lifts my chin to look at him again.

"Don't be shy to look at me, Maya. It turns me on that you'd want to check me out."

He stands with his feet apart and gives me a slow spin.

"You must know I'm always looking at you, too."

I can feel the color rise in my face but I force myself to look him up and down before lingering on his cock. My stare seems to make it harden. He's well-groomed, with a small thatch of hair surrounding the base of his dick and no hair elsewhere. His dick curves up and slightly to the left, thick and beautifully veiny. His foreskin sits tightly around his head, which juts out like an unripe plum, glistening with fresh precum. I bite my lip.

"If you keep looking at me like that, I'm going to fuck you right here against the wall and wine will have to wait again." His words are both a threat and a dare. I love making him growl.

Without thinking, I reach for him and my fingers close around his girth. I hum in appreciation; I know exactly how great this cock can make a woman feel. Adam puts his hand on top, seemingly to stop me, before closing around mine instead.

He moves my hand up and down and I step closer; close enough to bite his shoulder and hear him swear under his breath.

"Damnit, Maya...Uh...oh...Are you not going to...let me fuck you again?" His voice sounds pained, but he's not desperate enough; not like I am for him.

"Hmm. I don't know. I really enjoy ignoring your little warnings." He starts to chuckle but stops when I tighten my grip and increase my speed. He tries to slow my hand, but I resist.

"God, Maya...Didn't I...Didn't I make you feel good? When I was inside you?" My hands slow as I remember our union earlier and he seizes the opportunity to reach for my kitty. She started purring once I opened the bathroom door, and now my wetness is slowly dripping down my inner thigh.

"When I pushed into you and hit you in exactly the right spot?" To demonstrate, he presses his middle finger firmly against my g-spot, his thumb rubbing against my clit. I can feel the ridges of his fingerprint against my sex and widen my stance.

"Mmmm. You definitely...make me feel...gooooood." I stretch the word out involuntarily when he adds another finger to my pussy, pumping in and out. Who fucking knows what happened to that wine. That thought pulls me out of my sex haze enough to remember I'm trying to gain some semblance of control. Right now, it feels like he's John Legend and I'm just a piano. I re-tighten my grip, shrug his hand off mine, and stroke him with torturously perfect pressure. His thigh muscles flex and his chest huffs from the effort of resisting his release.

"Maybe if you beg," I taunt. His midnight eyes consume me and he pushes his fingers harder against my g-spot in a deep thrust.

"Please." *Oh my goodness!* I have to clench my jaw and focus on breathing deeply not to cry out. A few breaths later, I regain my composure...barely.

"Please what?" I try to smile, but I can feel my lips quivering with need. He begins making a come hither gesture with the fingers inside me and I'm forced to release my grip on his cock and clutch his shoulders for balance. He smiles at me like the cat who ate the canary.

"Please let me fuck you, Maya." Thankfully, he withdraws from me before I cum and end my very short stint as a dominatrix. I simply nod, unable to trust my voice.

He takes me by the wrist and marches me back into the bedroom. Rather than pull the sheets back, he bends me over the bed, nudging my feet wider so he can stand between them. I know what's coming, so I arch my back for a better angle. He quickly sheaths himself and kisses my opening with the tip of his shaft.

"I never would've guessed a nice girl like you would make me beg." He caresses my ass in light circles, raising goosebumps all over my body.

"Who said I was nice?" My voice is breathy. I can't keep hiding how crazy he's driving me.

"Oh, you're very nice." And with that, he takes hold of my hips and pushes into me a single inch. He flexes his hips again and again, pumping inside me shallowly. Every time I push back against him to deepen his penetration, he pulls back to prevent it. I practically grunt in frustration.

"Goddammit, Adam. Fuck me already!" He lets out a wicked laugh and deepens his stroke...but not deep enough.

"Mmm. Maybe you are naughty after all." He smacks my butt then smooths the sharp pain with a sensual pet. The unexpected sensation causes me to tighten around him and he pushes in another inch. He still denies me, refusing to fill me all the way.

Taking matters into my own hands (literally), I reach between my legs to massage his balls; they are drawn tight and feel heavy in my palm. I push back while he's distracted until he's fully embedded inside me. My pussy is stretched tightly around his cock and I feel his thighs on the back of my ass.

"Tsk tsk tsk. So impatient!" His voice is mocking, but he starts a steady rhythm in and out of my streaming cunt. I feel like I'm burning, like my nerve endings are being stripped bare and raw. Sex with Adam is so intense, so heated, so wanton.

My hands grasp the sheets tightly and my thighs begin to tremble.

"Adam. God, I'm so close." He picks up the pace and reaches around to rub my clit. I shake my head vehemently side to side, the pleasure overwhelming.

"Cum for me, Maya. I want to feel you go molten on my dick. No one's ever been this tight, this hot. Cum for me!"

I follow his instructions and shatter around his cock, my senses reeling. Several strokes later, I feel the telltale jerk of his hips as he cums, filling the condom with his warm ejaculation. We both are breathing like we've just run a race.

Fully spent, I let myself drop down to the bed and snuggle into the sheets, the exertion seeping into my muscles. He nudges me further onto the bed and pulls the sheets over us before spooning behind me. One arm is wrapped possessively around my waist. I cuddle closer against him before a sudden realization hits me right in the chest: we've just made love.

CHAPTER TWENTY-ONE

Adam

Maya watches the city pass through the window of the cab, and I pull her tighter against my side. Tonight, I'm taking her to my favorite place in all of New York City: Brooklyn Bowl. I've always been shit at bowling, but the food is amazing (where else can you eat falafel and blackened salmon and bowl at the same time?) and the live bands are stellar. Eric gifted me two tickets for The Roots when his sitter fell through, and Maya was my automatic plus one. If his taste in everything else is as good as his taste in music, Eric might graduate from "work friend" to "real friend" soon.

Things with Maya have been incredible. It's been four weeks since we made things official, and every time together is just as erotic as the first. The morning after her surprise seduction, I woke her up early to leave my stamp on her pussy twice more; once with her knees flung over my shoulders, buried deep inside her as I rubbed her clit until she spoke in tongues, and again in the shower, our lovemaking fogging up the glass way more than steam ever could. I never even thought about setting a timer for cuddling.

Ravenous, we ordered delivery from the deli across the street before taking a train downtown and walking the Highline all afternoon. We talked about everything, from why she left her hedge fund job to finally follow her passion, to how close I am with my brothers and the friendly rivalry between my dad, Noah, and Henry, Jr., the lawyers of the family.

Ever since, we've been alternating between my place in Bushwick and her place in Fort Greene, spending almost every night together. There's never enough time before I have to leave for work or she has to get home to feed Kahn. During our sleepovers, I discovered that she can be a bit bossy in the bedroom, and that I'm more than happy to follow her orders.

"So, have you been to Brooklyn Bowl before?" I can only see her silhouette in the darkness of the cab, punctuated by the red and green of traffic lights. She turns to me and smiles.

"Actually no. Because I value my time and safety, I've made a point of avoiding any place that can only be reached via the G train." She absently puts her hand on my leg and I silently thank God I suggested we take a cab instead of the subway to hide my reaction to her.

"Well, Ms. Smart Aleck, you're in for a treat. I used to sneak out to see bands play here all through high school. And I caught a show every trip home during college."

"Wow. I really had you pegged from the beginning. Did you wear any of your fedoras when you snuck out?" I can't see the mischievousness in her eyes, but I can certainly hear it in her tone. It might be time I come to terms with being a hipster. I tickle her in the spot behind her knee and she can't help but squeal with laughter. I keep firm hold of her hips when she attempts to squirm away.

"Oh yeah? We're doing that? OK!" She tries to tickle me on my side but is thwarted by my flannel and t-shirt, which dampen her efforts. She huffs in mock frustration before inclining her head and kissing along my neck. My dick goes from semi-hard to steel in two seconds flat.

"Uh huh. You may not be that ticklish, but I can still get a rise out of you." She kisses more deeply and even sucks my earlobe.

"Maya," I whisper so the driver won't hear. "How am I supposed to get out if you have me standing at full attention when we get there?" She just laughs and moves to my other ear. I close my eyes in pleasure.

"That sounds like a *you* problem, Adam." She loves getting me riled up and then making me beg for it. I cast a nervous glance at the driver before deciding Mohammed has probably seen way worse in the back of his cab. I pull Maya into my lap and kiss all over her cleavage before plundering her mouth. She tastes like cinnamon gum and her own unique flavor. As usual, I can't get enough.

"Two can definitely play that game, Maya," I say against her lips.

I tangle my fingers in her locs (which she wore down tonight, at my request), tilting her head for better access to her mouth. She's pushing her tits against me and I move my hand up her shirt to squeeze them but stop myself in the knick of time.

"Wait, wait," I pant, pulling away to rest my forehead on hers. "We're about to start something we can't finish here."

If my dick had legs, it would kick my ass right now. It'd also probably run to Maya's house and beg to move in. Both of us are breathing heavily, but calmer heads prevail and she reluctantly slides off my lap to sit next to me. She keeps her hand on my thigh, though.

"Sorry. You're right. You just make me so horny some-times." I take her hand, intertwining our fingers.

"The feeling is mutual, baby." *Very fucking mutual.* She might be the first woman whose sex drive has matched mine.

I feel the cab start to slow and spot the marquee in the distance. It looks like we stopped just in time.

Maya is so terrible at bowling, I would feel bad if she weren't such a good sport. All night, I've gotten to watch her waddle up to the lane, bend over, and granny roll her ball down the lane. Even the people in the booth next to us snickered when she acted like she'd won gold at the Olympics after knocking down just three pins. She's so goddamn cute it hurts. This time, her ball slowly drops into the gutter, all her pins still upright.

"You know, I could have them put up the bumpers, if you like." She turns around with fire and passion in her eyes, letting me know my jokes won't go unpunished. Of course, punishment for her means either I have to give her a massage, or she gets to pick where we eat for dinner. She hasn't figured out that, since my massages work like foreplay, I might be goading her on intentionally...just a little.

"And who are you? The Big Lebowski?"

"Solid reference, baby. Maybe watching some more bowling movies will improve your game." She smiles and playfully punches my arm.

"Alright. Your turn."

I bowl a decent seven while Maya sips her spicy margarita. As I walk back to our booth, she looks at me with a thoughtful expression on her face.

"What's up, babe?" She puts her drink down and turns to face me.

"I really like you, Adam." *That's it?* I thought it was obvious we like each other, even just based on the cab ride here. But she seems so earnest in her admission, I have to respond.

"I really like you too, Maya." She takes both of my hands in hers and kisses my knuckles before taking a deep breath. Oh God. What is she leading up to?

"I want you to meet my friends." My heart resumes beating; Maya seems completely unfazed.

"Wow. Are we talking about Tiffany and Denise?" She and her girlfriends are close. More than once, a text from one of them has woken me up in the middle of the night when she forgot to put her phone on silent. One of those times, I saw something about "skipping girls' night to get some Dubu dick" and almost died laughing. These chicks seem pretty cool to me.

"Yep. They said I've had you to myself for long enough and they need to meet the guy who was worth taking the train back early for."

"That sounds great. Of course I want to meet them." I give her a kiss on the cheek and nudge her to take her turn. "Where and when?" Maya bowls another goose egg and laughs at herself; I continue to enjoy the view as she bends over to roll the ball. She turns back to me, chagrined.

"Does brunch tomorrow sound OK? I know family dinner is Sunday evenings, so I'm hoping that works." She looks nervous for my answer and I don't hesitate to reassure her.

"Of course that works. Will mimosas be involved?"

"You know it."

I wait to feel nervous about meeting her friends, but the dread never comes. Everything with Maya just seems natural. Even little things like holding hands and sharing dessert. I put that idea aside and order another round of drinks. Heavy thoughts can wait; tonight is all about fun.

CHAPTER TWENTY-TWO

Maya

It's lucky I made a reservation because Chez Ma Tante is packed today. I shouldn't be surprised, considering I picked the best brunch spot in the city. Tiffany and Denise appear to be engaged in a "battle of the boobs": Tiffany's wearing a skintight bodysuit in deep brown with a scandalous sweetheart neckline and a gold chain around her waist; while Denise is wearing a scarlet red top so low cut you can see her ribcage tattoo, with houndstooth capris and black platforms. In comparison, I look like a nun in a floral summer dress with a boat neckline.

"Y'all didn't tell me I was supposed to dress like one of the Real Housewives of Jersey Shore for this brunch." I sulk around the straw of my Bloody Mary and check the maitre'd podium for the fifth time. Tiffany waves her nude talons dismissively.

"Oh girl, stop. You look great. Plus, you've already caught a man. I'm still recruiting for the position." Denise laughs at Tiffany's boldness and drinks from her mimosa.

"And I'm not looking for a man, but my style is just too good to turn off." Denise and Tiffany tangle fingertips in bawdy camaraderie.

I begrudgingly smile at my two best friends. After years of only seeing Tiff around the holidays or the odd long weekend, I finally have both of my girls in one place for happy hour, karaoke, or the occasional "Binge & Bitch" session, where we binge a Netflix show while drinking wine and bitching about guys. I smile to myself, realizing I haven't needed one of those since I met Adam. And speaking of Adam, I look up to see the maitre'd directing him to our table.

My God, the man is hot. I may tease him about it, but he really can dress. Today, he's wearing a denim button down with tan jeans cuffed at the bottoms. His shirt is open enough to show a hint of chest hair, and he's wearing his ever present Converse All Stars. I'm not the only one who notices him walk in—I see a few women practically break their necks to get a look—but his eye contact with me is unwavering.

He makes his way through the crowded restaurant like a heat seeking missile locked on to my womanhood; my pussy actually gets wetter the closer he gets. I keep waiting for my intense attraction to Adam to wear off, but it just seems to increase the more I get to know him. Not only is he sinfully gorgeous, he's also a truly good person.

So what in the world does he see in me? I quickly shake those doubts aside. This brunch *will* be a success. Tiffany and Denise both sit up straighter once they realize Adam's approaching our table.

"Damn, girl! It's like *that*?" Tiffany mutters under her breath. *Yeah, it is.* I give her a wink and turn as Adam pulls out the empty chair.

"I'm so sorry I'm late. The train got held underground, otherwise I would have texted." He turns to me apologetically and kisses my cheek. I take his hand and squeeze it reassuringly.

"It's all good, babe. We just ordered some brunch cocktails to get started."

"Sounds good to me. So..." He looks between Denise and Tiffany. "Which one of you is Denise and which one is Tiffany?" Denise is the first to extend her hand for a handshake.

"I'm Denise. I've been friends with Maya since Pratt and we were even roommates for a year—"

"The worst idea ever," I interrupt. "Between your massive closet and my endless crafting supplies, we sometimes had trouble finding the couch." We both laugh and Tiffany takes Denise's hand out of Adam's and replaces it with her own.

"And I'm Tiffany. Maya and I have been tight since, like sixth grade?" I nod at Tiff. "She's also been filling in at my Summer program up in Harlem." Adam smiles warmly at both of my friends.

"Oh, I know all about that program. That's the reason Maya's alarm has been waking us up at 7:00 AM every Saturday." Adam gives me a heated look that reminds me what we're *really* doing when my alarm goes off and I avert my eyes so my friends don't see me blush profusely. While some prefer "afternoon delight", suffice it to say, Adam is a morning person.

"So you've been staying over a lot, have you?" Tiffany's eyebrow is raised and my face turns even brighter red. I *knew* they were going to embarrass me today! To my surprise, Adam scoots his chair closer to mine and puts his arm around me.

"As much as she'll let me. Her place has way better food, plus I hate when she has to leave early to feed Khan."

Denise and Tiffany exchange amused looks before the waiter thankfully interrupts their impending battery of questions. Denise and I get the pancakes and fennel sausage, Adam gets the egg and sausage sandwich, and Tiffany gets the quiche. In keeping with my promise, I also order mimosas for Adam and myself.

"So, Adam. *Staying over? Meeting the friends?* You must be getting serious about our friend here." *Tiffany is relentless!* I hide my face in my hands but not before seeing Denise smile and lean forward expectantly.

"Tiffany!" I squeal. I turn to Adam, my eyes pleading. "I'm so sorry, babe. I promise I didn't ask her to ask you that." Adam looks thoroughly entertained by this line of questioning.

"I don't mind." He takes a sip of his mimosa before turning to Tiffany. "To answer your question, yeah, Maya and I are definitely something special."

"Hmm," Tiffany looks unconvinced. "'Special'? Not 'Serious'?" I level Tiffany with my best withering stare. Adam laughs out loud.

"I'd hate to speak for Maya, so I'll leave that one alone." Tiffany opens her mouth to grill Adam further and I'm once again saved by the waiter who sets down our plates. I focus on eating and not the inquisition to avoid dying of embarrassment.

"I'm glad to hear you know how special Maya is." Denise chimes in for the first time since introductions. *Thank God!* I'm going to need to have a talk with Tiffany. "So, have you ever dated a Black woman before, Adam?" I clench my fork so hard it might snap.

"Denise!" Oh my God. Kill me now!

"What? I think it's a fair question." Of course Tiffany does. The two of them have practically no filter. I warned Adam beforehand, but they are in rare form today.

"You're right," Adam begins. "It is a fair question, especially from two people looking out for their friend." He smiles at me and squeezes my hand under the table. "No, I've never gone out with a Black woman before...I've never gone out with anyone like Maya before." Denise leans closer to Adam, the judgement clear in her eyes.

"And what exactly does that mean?" Denise asks. I know she means well, but the claws are definitely out. Adam takes a big bite of his sandwich; chewing while mulling over the question.

"Well, she's beautiful, of course. She's talented as hell." Adam makes a show of thinking. "She's a badass girl boss."

"My girl's definitely a boss; no qualifiers necessary," Tiffany insists. Adam nods, smart enough not to push the issue.

"No doubt. Maya's sweet, willing to do anything for a friend or loved one in need. And she's hella smart." Adam wipes his mouth before taking another bite of his sandwich. "I mean, I know she's way more than that, but that's just off the top of my head."

I'm stunned. He just said the sweetest things any guy has ever said to or about me, but he's acting like it was the most casual thing in the world. Both Denise and Tiffany have knowing smiles on their faces.

"That's all well and good," Denise continues, "but do you really know Maya? Like even her pet peeves, her dealbreakers?" Thank goodness Adam is a good sport. They are not going easy on him.

"For Maya, cheating is a dealbreaker," offers Denise.

"Noted, though I think that's true for most people." He looks me in the eyes directly. "Cheating has never been my style." I sigh in relief. The girls might be a bit nosy, but they're also asking questions I've been too scared to consider.

"And she hates when people order for her," Tiffany adds. "I totally get it. I could *never* let a guy order for me—"

"While I think it can be sexy when a man takes charge like that," Denise finishes. "And what about her favorite color?" Denise asks. Adam stays quiet, happy to watch my two best friends bust my chops. Tiffany interjects.

"She might tell you it's teal or maybe red, but in her heart of hearts, Maya's favorite color is—"

"Pink!" Denise yells triumphantly, a smug grin on her face. "Like Barbie pink. Seriously, she's got a closet full of the stuff, that she thinks we don't know about."

My cheeks turn that same shade and I slouch in my seat.

"Guys," I pout. "Can't a girl have a few guilty pleasures without her girls ratting her out to her boyfriend?" They just smile and Adam has the nerve to chuckle. Tiffany puts her fork down, her expression serious.

"If I'm being real though, I wanna warn you that race *will* come up at some point. I see it all the time at my school. The kids are young, but a lot of the time, it's the same shit we're dealing with." She takes a sip of her Bloody Mary. "Dealing with the race bullshit, the discrimination, may not be fun, but it's best to face it head on." Her face turns even more solemn. "And *believe her*...if she talks to you about it."

The whole table is quiet for a moment. There's clearly a story behind Tiffany's words, but I doubt she'd want to get into it in front of Adam. I make a mental note to talk to her about it soon. Adam finishes his sandwich and puts his hand on my thigh under the table.

"Thanks for the insight, ladies." He gives my thigh a squeeze. "Seems like we blew right past small talk, which is fine by me."

"In the words of Sweet Brown," starts Denise, "'ain't nobody got time for that.'" She raises her glass and Tiffany giggles and clinks her glass to Denise's.

I'd been avoiding this conversation,—even in 2024, we can't kid ourselves that being together won't rub some people the wrong way—but it was relatively painless. Tiffany is right; it's best to face this head on.

For the rest of the meal, Tiffany and Denise thankfully stick to more traditional interrogation topics. Tiffany asks about Adam's job and educational background, while Denise asks about his family and exes before I shut down that conversation. I don't need Adam thinking about his exes any more than absolutely necessary.

Other than the initial questions about race and relationship status, this may have been the most successful "meet the friends" outing I've ever had. Adam fits right in and doesn't shy away from the tough conversations. By the time the check comes, we're even talking about another brunch date. Maybe Adam and I *are* starting to get serious.

CHAPTER TWENTY-THREE

Adam

I look down at the legal pad in front of me and see a crude doodle of a woman's face with long, flowing locs in the margin of my notes. It's safe to say I could never have gotten into Pratt with these skills. At the time, I was busy "sowing my wild oats" on the other side of the country. If I had met Maya then, like when I was home on break or something, would I have hit on her?

I pride myself on being a smart guy, but I was practically drowning in interested women in college. Women who let themselves into my room while I was in class. Women who installed viruses on their computer just so I could fix it. Even multiple women at the same time, hoping to check "college threesome" off their bucket list. Honestly, I doubt I would've seen Maya through all that...noise.

Next to me, Eric clears his throat and nudges my foot under the table. The room of my colleagues looks at me expectantly. *Busted.*

"I'm sorry," I say, chagrined. "I was reviewing my notes and missed what you said. Could you please repeat that?" Mr. Hallorann, my boss and a little bit of a hardass, leans forward in his chair at the head of the conference room table.

"How is the migration coming, Adam? It's critical that our transition to RISE goes off without a hitch." Right. The migration. That has only been my top priority for the past three months. Luckily, I can talk about that project in my sleep if necessary.

"It's going well, sir. We are on track to finish on the 31st of next month, as projected." Mr. Hallorann steeples his fingers on the desk and smiles approvingly.

"Great work, Adam. I knew you'd stay on top of it." He stacks his papers emphatically. "Lets give everyone back," he looks at his watch, "eleven minutes of their time."

The meeting adjourned, everyone gathers their things and starts to clear out of the room. Eric gestures to my notepad as he shoves his laptop into his bag.

"Is that her?" I raise an eyebrow inquisitively.

"Is that who?" Eric gives me a smug smirk like he thinks I'm an idiot.

"Who? The girl that's got you zoning out in status meetings, that's who." We both walk out of the conference room and head in the direction of the kitchen. I sigh, knowing I've got no choice but to spill the beans.

"Yes, that's Maya. Though my lack of drawing skills definitely doesn't do her justice." We reach the kitchen, and Eric grabs one of the bagels someone brought in this morning. By the afternoon, only pumpernickel and onion are left, and there's no cream cheese. *Pass.* Eric clearly doesn't share my reservations; he takes a big bite of the pumpernickel bagel...raw. I try to hide my grimace.

"Hey. Don't judge me. I had to work through lunch to prepare for that meeting you just slept through." I raise my hands in defense. Someone's feeling fiesty today.

"Whoa, whoa, man. I tuned out for like a minute. Plus, I think I recovered pretty quickly." Eric sighs and wipes his hand down his face. He looks exhausted.

"Sorry, man." He sits down at one of the tables and I pull up a chair. "Sarah, our youngest, has strep...*again*. I was in urgent care and then we were up all night until her fever broke."

"That sounds awful. Is she feeling any better today?" Eric lets out a mirthless laugh.

"That's just it; she's feeling great now. After finally passing out at 5:00 AM and sleeping for six hours, she woke up fully rested like nothing even happened. Meredith is home with her and apparently Sarah's nonstop energy is driving her insane." I chuckle before I can hide my amusement with a cough. Eric takes another bite of untoasted bagel.

"Laugh all you want, but someday, maybe with this Maya woman, you will know my pain." Two months ago, that comment alone would have sent my running for the hills. Now...?

"Maya and I are hardly *there* yet, but thanks for the vote of confidence." Eric stops chewing and stares at me. "What?"

"Adam Park just used the word 'yet' about becoming a parent, that's what." Eric feels his forehead worriedly. "Maybe I'm coming down with strep and this whole conversation is just a fever dream." I stand up to put some distance between myself and patient zero.

"Don't tell me you came into work today contagious, Eric." Eric ponders that thought before resuming his bagel "meal".

"No...I don't think so...Hmmm." Eric feels the back of his neck. "You know what? I'll take a Z-pack just in case." I take another step back.

"Nice. Why don't you call it a day before you cause an outbreak at the office." Eric shrugs and grabs his things.

"You don't have to tell me twice." He polishes off his bagel, the last bite still in his mouth as he talks. "Once I'm home, I'm happy to spitball proposal ideas for that Maya girl if you want." My eyes widen in shock.

"Go ahead and stop by urgent care, Eric. You're clearly delusional."

Eric just smirks and waves as he heads for the elevators. To think that Maya and I are that serious after just a couple months. That's ridiculous...right?

In my right hand, I've got an English cucumber, and in my left, your garden variety cucumber. I step closer to Maya to avoid the teenagers playing bumper cars with their shopping cart. It's a madhouse in here.

"Maya! Which one?" Maya looks up from the pineapples to inspect the cucumbers I'm holding. She's got a wicked gleam in her eye.

"Hmmm." She walks slowly over to me and takes each cucumber in her hand. She makes a point of squeezing and stroking both while looking me in the eyes. "I like this one," she says of the English cucumber. "It's nice and *long*...and *thick*. It looks like it'll be a really...satisfying mouthful." At the last innuendo, Maya can't contain her laughter and starts giggling like a schoolgirl. The mom of the teenagers raises an eyebrow and shoos her kids along.

"Sorry!" I yell after her. "She really loves salad!" This sends Maya into another fit of laughter.

"You're going to get us kicked out of Trader Joe's if you keep this up." I pull her closer to me and move her locs aside to plant a kiss on her neck. She's warm and breathes out a little sigh that lets me know she likes what I'm doing. Even in public, she's so responsive to me.

"How much more do you need, babe. We should've gotten a cart." She smiles, a little embarrassed.

"You know how I get in TJ's. My shopping list goes out the window. Let's get a bottle of rosé and we can call it done. This is going to be delicious." I take her hand as we walk to the wine section.

"Deal. I can hardly complain when I'm getting another delicious meal out of it. Though, in fairness, every meal you make is delicious." She squeezes my hand gently and pulls me toward the bottles.

Maya comes out of the kitchen with a plate of lemon bars and sits next to me on the couch. Her soft hips mold perfectly against my body.

"Ribeye, fancy wine, and now lemon bars? What's the occasion?" She shifts to put her legs in my lap before grabbing the remote.

"Nothing really. I just like to show off sometimes...And..." She bites her lip, suddenly nervous. "I also want to thank you for being so cool at brunch last weekend. My girlfriends really gave you the third degree." I lean down and kiss her nose.

"You're adorable when you're nervous, but you have no reason to be. I said I had fun and I meant it."

Seemingly satisfied with my answer, Maya turns towards the TV to find our evening entertainment. For some reason, she looks especially beautiful tonight. Her hair is down, her pink tank top is showing off her collar bones and breasts, and her short polka dot skirt is barely covering her bottom.

Maya browses her watchlist, but I can't stop thinking about that word. "Yet". Maya and I weren't to the point of having kids YET. Eric definitely caught me off guard with that comment, but alarm bells still aren't sounding in my head. Maybe Maya is the real deal. Maybe realizing she's the real deal is why she's so irresistible tonight. Maybe it's time to take things to the next step and see for real if we sink or swim. But first, I ought to give some attention to the beautiful woman in front of me.

My dick twitches under her smooth legs and I can't help rubbing them. I love the way my hands look against her dark skin. It makes making love to her even more erotic. While my left hand keeps stroking her legs—moving from her ankles to the hem of her tiny skirt and back down—, my right slips under her shirt to undo the clasp of her bra. The straps fall down her shoulders and she turns towards me. The arousal in her eyes is clear.

"Did you change your mind about checking out 'Squid Game' with me?" I pull the straps down her arms and slip the bra from under her shirt. Her nipples are already hard.

"I'll take that as a 'yes'." I nod and move my left hand to between her legs. She spreads her legs to give me better access.

"Who would've thought that a ribeye and roast potatoes was an aphrodisiac?" she ponders aloud. I stop briefly and look into her eyes.

"Are you serious? Steak for a guy is like chocolate covered strawberries for a woman." She presses her lips together to keep from laughing and I resume caressing her skin and her cute pink panties. I move further down the couch and position myself between her legs.

"Earlier, you mentioned something about a 'satisfying mouthful'." I reach under her skirt to the waistband of her panties and she lifts up her hips so I can remove them. I smell her flower and lean forward to take a deep breath. Goosebumps appear on her thighs.

"Adam!" She covers her face bashfully but doesn't close her legs. I kiss down her thighs and see the wetness easing out of her pussy. I lean further down and lick slowly from her seeping opening to her eager clit. Her skirt is bunched around her generous hips and her nipples are straining against the thin fabric of her shirt; she is the epitome of sex.

I take her clit in between my lips and hum to send vibrations through her. Her hips buck hard and I reach under her ass to hold her in place.

"Don't go anywhere, baby." I hum again against her clit and smooth her juices up and down her seam with my index finger. Her hips strain against my grip, but she stays in place.

"Holy shit, Adam. *This* is new." I run my fingers up from her opening, around her clit, and back down, over and over again.

"What can I say? I like to try new things." I keep humming on her clit while rubbing around her pussy, driving her crazy with need. I don't penetrate her, enjoying teasing her as long as possible before granting her release. Her hand moves to the back of my head to force the issue, but I shake it off and continue my torture.

"Fuck, Adam! This feels sooooooo goood...Uhmmm...But are you not going to let me cum?" I smile against her lips and finger her opening without pushing in.

"In time. I'm really enjoying *this* at the moment." Her pussy is dripping for me now, and I push my finger further inside her. She starts straining even harder against my grip.

"God, Adam. I'm so fucking close. Please!" Once I hear the magic word, I cover her clit fully with my mouth, vigorously move my finger in and out of her wet passage, and press down on her mound to add pressure and push her over the edge. She explodes, flooding my mouth with her essence and screaming so loud I hear Khan run to the bedroom. Apparently we had an audience.

Her legs keep quivering as the aftershocks flow through her, and she pushes me off, the pleasure too intense. Both of us are sweaty and breathing hard. I rest my head on the inside of her leg. She lazily runs her fingers through my hair as she comes down.

"Will you come to dinner with my family this Sunday?" I ask, still out of breath. Her strokes stop abruptly and she sits up on her elbows.

"What?" I lift my head and look her in the eyes.

"Would you come to my parent's house this Sunday to meet everyone? All my brothers are going to be there and it's a big celebration before Damon has to go back overseas." She blinks a few times, her expression unreadable.

"Did you really just ask me to come meet your parents with your head between my legs?" She cracks a small smile and I smile in return.

"I figured you'd be in a good mood, so you wouldn't say 'no'." She puts her feet on the floor and faces me, a serious look on her face. Uh-oh.

"Adam Park, I would love to meet your family." I pull her in for a hug, my heart nearly beating out of my chest. "And just so you know, I would've said yes even without the...dessert," she blushes, "though I did enjoy it."

With that weight off my chest, I pick her up and carry her to the bedroom to finish what I started.

CHAPTER TWENTY-FOUR

Maya

Things have been going so well with Adam. I mean...like *fantastic*. He gets along with my friends, we both love spending time together, and we *definitely* click sexually. It's so amazing, in fact, that I keep waiting for the other shoe to drop. How could I meet this smart, sexy family man and he's actually into me as much as I'm into him? I'm so used to pulling more than my weight in a relationship and being with Adam feels like...a relief. Like when you take off your bra after a long day and now you just let yourself hang free. Like when you finally get your dream job after countless rounds of interviews and now that you're on your new team, everything just clicks.

And now, after only a couple of months, we've reached a milestone: I'm going to meet his family. Before Damon goes back to start the season in Portugal, they're having a going away dinner and Adam invited *me*. "Little Ms. Nappy Head" herself is getting serious with a Korean hottie from a good family with a great job, so Jenny Craig, Weight Watchers, and Slim-Fast can all *kiss my ass*.

I'm excited to meet them, but also beyond nervous about making a good impression, especially with his parents. From what Adam's told me, his dad can be a bit old school; his mom even quit working when they got married. *What if she thinks I'm trying to steal away her baby boy? What if tonight turns into the latest remake of "Guest Who's Coming to Dinner"? What if, what if, what if....*

I wipe my sweaty palms against the pashmina over my silk blouse and navy pencil skirt and tighten my grip on the wine I brought. Adam said it's his father's favorite. For his mother, I brought a colorful bouquet of lilacs and hydrangeas that's peaking out of my leather tote. My home training would never allow me to show up empty-handed, even if Adam promised I didn't need to bring anything.

I ring the doorbell of the Clinton Hill brownstone and wish for the umpteenth time that Adam and I could have come together. He had a presentation late this afternoon and said meeting here would be fine...but what if I beat him here? What did he tell his family about me? Oh gosh, I don't think I can–

Right then, Adam's mother opens the door, a welcoming smile on her face.

"Well, hello!" she almost sings. "You must be Maya!" She pulls me in for a warm hug and I feel my shoulders relax a bit. She steps back to let me inside and my heart sinks when I realize Adam isn't here.

"Come in! Come in! And what have you brought?" I release my death grip on the wine and dig into my purse for the flowers.

"Just some wine...and some flowers for you. I hope you like them." My nerves are making it hard to speak above a whisper. Adam's mom brings the flowers up to her nose and inhales deeply.

"I love them and they smell just lovely. Henry?!" She inclines her head and yells to Adam's dad who must be upstairs. "Maya's here and she brought that wine you like!"

She turns back to me and gently grabs my elbow, leading me towards the kitchen.

"Now let's get these in some water."

Their kitchen is bright and colorful and appears to be fully stocked courtesy of Whole Foods and Dean & Deluca. What I wouldn't give to attempt a croquembouche with the full set of Lagostina Martellata cookware like the one I see hanging above the kitchen island. I am in heaven!

"Your home is beautiful, Mrs. Park," I say as I spot marble countertops and even a window overlooking an herb garden in the backyard.

"Please. Call me Marie." I nod automatically, knowing full well I'll never call Adam's mom by her first name. I lean against the counter and gesture vaguely.

"Can I help you with anything in here?" She shakes her head, focused on arranging my bouquet in a crystal vase that looks like it cost more than my rent.

"You're our guest. The only thing I need you to do is head into the dining room and pour yourself a glass of wine. Alex just texted that he's walking from the train."

I walk down the hall in the direction of men laughing and find Adam's brothers enthusiastically discussing the latest Giants loss and hoarding all the salami from the charcuterie board. They all turn as I enter the room. The twins both stand.

"Hi!" they say at the same time.

"Hi. I'm Maya. And you must be...?"

"I'm Henry, Jr.," the one with the horn-rimmed glasses says. According to Adam, he's a tad formal and the most like their father. I extend my hand and he shakes it firmly.

"And I'm Noah." Noah is wearing pinstripe pants and a french cuff dress shirt like he came straight from the board-room to be here. His smile is genuine when I shake his hand. The super tall one stands up and stretches out his hand to shake mine.

"I'm Damon," he says, his mouth still partially full of salami. I smile shyly.

"I could've guessed, what with how tall you are." He smiles and sits back down before grabbing a handful of grapes.

The last brother is some sort of finance wizard, wearing jeans, a dress shirt, and a Patagonia vest. He didn't stand or smile when

I came into the room. The other brothers look at each other. Noah chimes in.

"And that's Cory. He must've been away when Mom and Dad taught the rest of us manners." Cory rolls his eyes, pours himself a glass of wine, and says nothing. That doesn't seem good.

The doorbell sends Mrs. Park running past us.

"That must be Adam!" I hear the door open and close and Adam and his mom greet each other. He comes into the dining room looking mesmerizing as usual: he's wearing a dark gray suit with a loosened tie around his neck and he's shaved off his stubble (probably for the presentation). He hangs his jacket on the chair next to mine and gives me a sweet kiss before hugging and greeting his brothers.

"What's up, everyone?" Adam gestures to me. "Have you all met Maya?" Henry, Jr. smiles in response.

"We just did. Adam, you never told us you were seeing such a beautiful woman." My cheeks redden and Adam beams with pride. He sits down next to me and takes my hand into his lap. He looks into my eyes.

"She's definitely something special." The butterflies already fluttering in my stomach from nerves are now pterodactyls. Cory snorts rudely.

"She's 'something' alright." Though he says it under his breath, Adam's grasp on my hand tightens painfully. He clearly heard it. Before the situation escalates, Adam's father walks into the room. No one else stands, so I keep my seat.

"Maya? This is my dad." His dad is tall, perhaps 6'2" or 6'3". That must be where Damon got his height. He's built like he used to be in the military, and keeps his hair cut very short. He's even more intimidating than his picture indicated and I gulp, but he surprises me by coming around to my chair and pulling me up for a hug.

"Hello, Maya. Adam has told us so much about you."

"He has?" I squeak. He lets me go and takes his seat at the head of the table then looks at me like I've sprouted a second head.

"Of course he has. Why wouldn't he tell us about the woman who stole his heart?" Adam abruptly starts coughing and pours himself a glass of wine. I hear his brothers snickering, even Henry, Jr.

Though his actions show he cares for me, Adam has yet to use the L word. I'm beautiful. I'm amazing. I'm bewitching. But he doesn't *love* me. I haven't "stolen his heart".

I, on the other hand, am head over heels for Adam and have been, maybe since that first night on the phone. He listens to me, he excites me, he just...gets me. No matter what we're doing, I enjoy being with him. Once I'm sure he feels the same way, I'll tell him I love him every day and twice on Sundays.

Adam's mom comes in with a roast turkey and Henry clears the charcuterie board to make room.

"Now that everyone's here, we can eat. Boys, can you grab the sides from the kitchen?"

CHAPTER TWENTY-FIVE

Adam

M om has always been a great cook, but she pulled out all the stops for Damon's going away party. I use my roll to sop up the extra gravy on my plate, though I seriously considered just licking it clean. Cory had more than considered it, hence why he's now wiping gravy off his chin with a dinner napkin.

He's been weird all night and it's really pissing me off. Maya's looking especially stunning tonight, and every chance he gets, Cory's been saying something snide about her under his breath.

"What's so special about you that you got my brother to change his ways?"

"So why'd you leave your real job to get into sewing?"

"You're nothing like the women my brother usually goes for."

"Oh, you went to Pratt? That's cool if you've got the talent to make a living doing art."

Maya had taken it like a champ, but I was so mad I had to let go of her hand or I would've broken her fingers. The others noticed too, but no one wanted to spoil Damon's big night. My mom puts another slice of turkey on Dad's plate.

"You know, Adam. This Maya girl you brought home is great...except for the fact that she keeps calling me Mrs. Park." Maya lowers her eyes and tries to hide her smile by pressing her lips together. I squeeze her thigh gently.

"Yeah, she does that. Don't worry. She'll start to relax after a few more hours." Cory sucks his teeth.

"Two months of dating and already he's a Maya expert," Cory mutters. He barely lowered his voice this time and I scoot my chair out from the table about to punch my bother in his dumb face, but Maya quickly grabs my hand and shakes her head slightly. Mom and Dad are shooting daggers are Cory, who's suddenly very interested in his potatoes.

"I'd say it's time for dessert," Mom interjects, always first to try to deescalate a "battle of the bros". Dad coined the term when Henry Jr. and Noah had both asked Madeleine Pinkett to Homecoming their sophomore year in high school. They even asked on the same day, though Noah picked lunch and Henry Jr. waited until the pep rally. That night at home, they both ended up with black eyes. After all that, Madeleine went with Noah (he *did* ask first), but left early to make out with Jeff Michaels under the bleachers. We don't argue much—not seriously, anyway—but when it happens, it tends to require outside intervention.

"Cory? How about you grab the brownies and ice cream from the kitchen?"

There is no way I'm letting Cory continue to disrespect Maya. I follow him to the kitchen when my mom sends him for dessert. Once out of earshot, I round on him.

"Hey Cory. What the fuck is your problem, man?" He pivots to face me and looks almost bored. That makes me even angrier and I clench my fists at my sides to keep from socking him in the jaw.

"No problem here, bro." I can see the anger in his eyes behind the feigned boredom.

"Why the hell have you been being so rude to Maya all night? Saying all that stupid shit under your breath. We can hear you." I fight to keep from yelling. "*Maya* can hear you." Cory rolls his eyes.

"After all the grade A women you've been with, I didn't expect you to bring a girl like her home to your family, that's all." I'm so mad I'm actually starting to get hot.

"You wanna tell me what you mean by that?" I ask through clenched teeth. Cory folds his arms over his chest.

"Don't play dumb, Adam. You know what I mean."

"I truly don't. Maya is smart and funny. She's super talented – you should see the ceramic stuff she makes – and super fun to hang out with. And she's got the biggest heart of anyone I know." Cory puts his hand up to stop me from gushing further.

"But not *beautiful*. Smart, kind, funny—sure. But you're telling me you'd really want her on your arm for celebratory drinks with your boss when you get that big promotion? You'd want to show her off in front of Bryan and his frat brothers? You'd really want to be seen at the beach with her?" Cory isn't hiding his anger now. Before I can tear Cory a new one, we both turn towards a noise behind us.

Maya is standing in the doorway. Her eyes are wet, but her jaw is high in defiance. She turns to face only me.

"Your mom sent me in to see what was taking so long with the dessert. I'll let her know you're on your way out." I see her lip quiver, but she doesn't let herself cry. Then she turns and heads back to the dining room before I can stop her. From the corner of my eye, I can see Cory looking thoroughly chastised. Good. I'm gonna do worse to him later.

Maya is noticeably quiet for the rest of the dinner. Thankfully, Cory has also stopped with his rude remarks. Maya won't let me hold her hand, though, and she's barely made eye contact since the kitchen, neither of which are a good sign.

With dessert and coffee done, we give hugs all around. Damon promises to call regularly and Mom and Dad invite Maya back for our annual Halloween party. I knew they would love her. Probably because of the incident in the kitchen, Maya says she'll try to make it. *Try.* Taking deep breaths to keep from hyperventilating, I hold the front door for Maya. On the street in front of Mom and Dad's place, she once again doesn't let me hold her hand.

"Maya. What's wrong baby?" She won't even look at me.

"You mean other than your brother being a jerk who apparently thinks I'm too ugly to even be in your life?" She'd kept her tears in check inside, but they fall freely now. Each one hitches the temperature of my blood up ten degrees hotter. I move to put my arms around Maya, the only woman I've *ever* asked to come to a family dinner, but she steps away. *Damnit, Cory!*

"Baby, I'm so sorry you heard what he said. He's an asshole."

"But he's not wrong," she sniffs. "...And you agree with him." OK. Now I'm pissed.

"I *agree* with him? Maya, what are you talking about?"

"If you'd thought I was beautiful, you would have said so." She imitates my voice. "'Maya is smart, funny, fun to be with, super talented.' But he was right; you *didn't* say I was beautiful." She's clutching her elbows now, and it's killing me she won't let me hold her.

"But I *do* think you're beautiful, Maya. I do! Just because I didn't say it, doesn't mean I don't think it." I can't stop myself from grasping her shoulders, hoping my message gets through. "You're beautiful!" She shakes her head, backing away.

"I'm gonna head home." Before I can take her hand, she adds, "*By myself.* I just need some space." Though she won't let me hold her hand, I start walking after her.

"Maya, c'mon! We need to talk about this! My brother is an asshole and he *does not speak for me*!!" She keeps walking, starting to turn away from me.

"Go back inside and talk to your brother, Adam. I don't want to be the reason you fight with your family." She turns completely now, walking off without looking back. She's running away...*again*.

She might not talk to me in person, but she *will* talk to me. I take my phone out and start dialing.

CHAPTER TWENTY-SIX

Maya

I lift my head up from my pillow to check my phone. Fifteen unread text messages. Twenty-five missed calls. Adam's been calling and texting me pretty much nonstop since I left his parent's place. I don't know what there is to say right now.

Tonight was truly a nightmare. I get up and start pacing, doing my best to walk out my frustrations.

First, I meet his parents and *all his brothers*—that's *four brothers*—by myself, since he's got some stupid fucking presentation. *Then* Cory turns out to be a major asshole, doing his best to make me feel small no matter what I said.

Oh, I don't have a real job, Cory? Tell that to my student debt! It's paid in full, bitch! *Oh, I'm nothing like Adam's other women?* That's a *good* thing, dumbass. Those hos never got to meet the family. Adam didn't give those skanks three orgasms just two nights ago!

I come to a dead stop at one horrible thought: Nothing Cory said hurt more than that Adam *doesn't* think I'm beautiful. It's all my deepest insecurities realized. Sure, he thinks I'm a good person, but I guess that's *in spite* of my looks? Another sob escapes my already sore throat and I drop back down on my bed and bury myself in the sheets.

Before I can fall asleep and pretend this whole night didn't happen, another call comes in. God, give it a rest! I grab my phone to silence it before I see who's calling; what a relief that it's Denise. I pick up immediately. A call will have to do until I can schedule a "Binge & Bitch" session. Denise doesn't bother with a greeting.

"Hey, girl!" she says cheerily. "Oh no, wait. Are you crying?" Denise's voice is so comforting I let my guard down and cry directly into the phone. I'm probably an ugly *crier* too.

"Adam," I sniff. "Adam thinks I'm ugly!" I let loose another wail and hear soothing tones over the line.

"C'mon, Maya. Calm down." She makes gentle shushing noises over the phone. Is my friend really trying to calm me down like a baby? Damn, it actually seems to be working, too.

"What you just said can't be true. Of course Adam doesn't think you're ugly. At brunch, he couldn't keep his eyes *or hands* off of you." It's hard to make out what she's saying over my crying, which has actually given me the hiccups.

"But he does." Even though I hate the whine creeping into my voice, I can't help it. "He just said I was fun, talented, and smart." The shushing sounds stop and now there's silence from Denise's side of the call. I hiccup, trying to get a hold of myself.

"Hello?" Maybe the phone went dead.

"...Uh, Maya?" Denise finally sighs. "Those are *good* things." I roll my eyes. Why is she being so thick-headed?

"Yeah, those are good things," I sniff, "but he didn't say I was *beautiful*. No woman wants her man to think she's got a" I use air quotes, though D can't see them, "'great personality' while secretly thinking she's a wildebeest! And his stupid brother, Cory, thinks I'm ugly too!" Even to my ears, I sound like a preteen brat. Denise just sighs. She's never had much patience.

"Maya, girl, you've gotta get over this." All soothing tones are gone from her voice. Instead, she sounds drained. "First, you thought Adam was too hot to like you. Then you thought he was just using you for some big-girl fetish." *Ha!* That thought, now, seems ridiculous.

"Then you decide to finally give it a shot with him, and you spend almost every day fucking like rabbits," she's picking up steam now, "but now, *now* you think he doesn't think you're attractive?" I feel like Denise just treated me as a hostile witness on one of those courtroom shows. *Your honor, I object!*

"Well...," I stammer. I don't have any response, but I also don't want her to keep yelling the truth at me. She ignores my feeble attempt to interrupt her.

"And it's not just with Adam. Despite the fact that you've had *several* long-term boyfriends, many of whom *you* dumped, you, for some reason, think all anyone sees when they look at you is some ugly, fat lady. And now you're using it to sabotage your relationship with Adam. You are not Precious! You've got a lot going for you, despite having the self esteem of a junior high kid." We're both silent, letting her words sink in. I can hear Denise breathing hard, like it took it out of her to release all that.

"How long have you been waiting to say that to me?" I ask quietly. From the sound of it, she's been holding that in for quite some time. After a moment, she laughs awkwardly.

"A while. Sorry. I didn't mean to unload on you." Now *I'm* the one that feels drained. Here l am, thinking I'm doing a great job hiding all my fears—all the nasty thoughts that whisper in my ear whenever I look in the mirror, all the self-doubt that makes me work so hard, trying to be good enough—and they've been in the driver's seat the whole time. It's so...embarrassing. And I feel so weak behind the ineffective facade.

"I'm sorry I'm not strong and confident like you," I practically whisper.

"Hey Maya. Why don't you shut the fuck up already?" D practically yells. I pull the phone away from my ear and stare at it, shocked.

"What?"

"You heard me," Denise returns angrily. "You think you're the only one with problems just because you're the one crying right now?"

"Well...no, of course not." This conversation is turning my already nightmarish night into a night terror.

"Some of us work with professionals for our issues instead of making our girlfriends listen to our sob stories, even when we have dreamy guys begging us to meet their families!" D's anger leaves me too stunned to speak.

"So that's it? Ten years of friendship and now I'm just some whiny bitch you're tired of listening to?"

"Your words, not mine, but if the shoe fits..." I can tell she's hurt even through the phone, but my feelings are too hurt to try to smooth things over.

"OK." I croak through more tears. "I guess we've said all there is to say." More silence.

"If that's how you feel..." I can hear her crying now. "I gotta go."

I hear the click as she ends the call and I feel completely shattered. Heartbroken by both Adam *and* one of my best friends! *How* dare *she take Adam's side!*

But I can't muster up the same anger as before. Why *did* I think Adam would agree with his brother? He's never given me any reason to doubt him before. And as mad as I am at Denise right now, she's right; I've never had any problem getting into a relationship. Why, then, is it so easy to believe Adam would agree with all the bullshit Cory was spewing?

Dammit! I can't believe I've been such a bonehead. I've got to call Denise back to make amends, but first I need to go to Adam's. He's right; we need to talk. And I might need to apologize.

Chapter Twenty-Seven

Adam

I'm starting to understand why this is the first time I've tried a relationship. Hookups are so much easier than this. There's no yelling, no tears, no misunderstandings. Well, there were sometimes misunderstandings when the women started to catch feelings...And sometimes there were tears when I let the women know those feelings weren't contagious. But that was on them; I was always honest from the start and never deviated.

Until Maya. Maya popped up in my chat window and has been surprising me ever since. I was surprised such a cute face was on the other side of the computer. I was surprised by how strongly I felt about her from the beginning. And now I'm surprised that she would just jump to the wrong conclusion without giving me a chance to explain. She's always running away!

I push up from the couch and slap myself in the face to end my solo pity party. *Man up, Adam! You're better than this.*

Getting my blood pumping always puts me in a better mood, so I start jogging in place. I do a few jumping jacks and burpees, trying to get it pumping even harder. This is bullshit! I've got a great job, an amazing apartment, a family that loves me, and I can bed any woman I want. I don't need M aya!

I stop jogging abruptly. No, I don't *need* Maya...but I *want* her. I flop back down on the couch and let out a groan of frustration. *God, it can't end like this.*

Ten minutes after I gave up calling, I hear my buzzer. Yes! That's probably Maya coming to make up in person. I knew we'd work it out. This was just our first fight. I may not be experienced with relationships, but I know fights are bound to happen. And I'm not going to throw in the towel at the first sign of trouble after waiting so long to dive into this. Maya is worth more than just a "college try".

I race over to the intercom on the wall to buzz her up. I almost fall flat on my ass when I slip on the entryway rug. *Real smooth, Adam.* Clearly, I'm too far gone to play it cool. I open the door and lean against the jamb to meet Maya with the best kiss of her life.

How in the fuck could she not *know* I think she's hot? I try to jump her bones every time I'm in a room with her, but I don't think she's beautiful? It's ridiculous. And Cory is an asshole. I'll gladly fuck her around the clock to erase any doubt from her mind about how much I'm into her. I've got some vacation time saved up. I guess we'll need to talk first, but...

One minute later, I get the shock of my life when strawberry blonde curls emerge on the stairs instead of Maya's dark locs. Shit. It's Emily. Could this night get any worse? I fold my arms over my chest. I am *not* in the mood for my friend's kid sister to make another pass at me. As the maid of honor, she's had entirely too much access to me. I'm *this* close to backing out of the *whole wedding*. As she gets closer, I see dark circles under her eyes. Several strands of hair have come loose from her ponytail. It's the first time I've ever seen her with even a hair out of place.

"Hey Adam" she mumbles, shuffling her feet along the floor. She looks like she hasn't slept in a while. Something is definitely up. "Do you have a minute to talk?"

My back is ramrod straight now and I step back into my apartment. "Now really isn't a good time, Emily. I'm kind of expecting—" She reaches her hand out, clearly worried I'll close the door in her face. I'd thought about it, but...

"Please, Adam? You've got every reason to want to avoid me, but I just want to talk. It's important." When I continue to hesitate, she pulls a bottle from her oversized purse and holds it out to me. "I brought wine?"

Damnit. I *really* don't need this tonight, but I'm pretty sure Bryan would kick my ass if I left her in this state. Against the niggling thoughts in the back of my head, I step aside to let her in.

"OK, Emily. You've got until I finish one glass of wine. What's up?" To ensure she knows my threat isn't idle, I move to the kitchen, grab a corkscrew, and immediately pour myself some wine while she settles on the couch. Her shoulders are hunched, and she's worrying her bottom lip between her teeth.

"First," she says, clearly about to launch into a prepared speech, "I want to apologize." I barely contain an eye roll. *This outta be good.*

"I know I've crossed the line through the years and..." she sighs. "I'm sorry. I know it wasn't cool."

"No, it really wasn't." I sit down a safe distance from her on the couch and sip my wine. "So...Was that it? I appreciate the apology, but you could've just texted."

Emily turns her knees towards me before looking up with tears in her eyes.

"Jesus, Emily," I curse, grabbing her hands in mine. They are cold and trembling. "What's wrong? Should I call Bryan?" The mention of her brother brings a panicked look to her eyes.

"No!" she shouts. "I'm not ready to tell him yet."

"Not ready to tell him what?" I ask, using the same tone you'd use around a loose wild animal. A tear trails down her cheek before she wipes it away with the edge of her shirt.

"The real reason I kept asking you out. Why I kept coming on so strong." I am beyond confused, my wine glass all but forgotten.

"I haven't told him you've hit on me, if that's what you're worried about. Assuming this apology means you won't do it again, what's the big deal?" She wipes her eyes again, but doesn't look up.

"I kept asking you out because I *knew* you would say no. I would ask you out, you would say no, and then I wouldn't have to think about who I *really* wanted, underneath the bullshit."

I grab my wine and gulp down half the crimson liquid at once, more confused than ever. She *wanted* me to say no?

"So who did you really want, then?"

Emily takes my hands in both of hers and looks me straight in the eyes.

"Women." She picks up my wine and empties the glass. "I'm attracted to women."

I jump up from the couch and head to the kitchen, bringing back another glass and the rest of the wine. She laughs lightly and pours herself a glass.

"That's big news, Em. How long have you known?" She takes another swig before answering, looking chagrinned.

"Maybe...Freshman orientation?" I playfully hit her with a pillow.

"Em! What the hell! Do you know how close I was to telling your brother about you hitting on me? You were really starting to make me uncomfortable." She winces around her glass and I pour more for myself.

"I know...I was terrible, wasn't I?" She pulls her ponytail out, before raking a hand through her hair. "I just...couldn't tell anyone. People in my industry talk. They think because their planner is gay suddenly they're going to have a 'gay wedding'."

"Oh, the horror!" I tease, clutching imaginary pearls. She cracks a smile at that. "I *maybe* get hiding it for work...*Maybe*," I grumble and eye her with suspicion. "I get not wanting to mess with your money. But do you really think Bryan is a homophobe? Do you think *I* am?" Her smile fades and I take her hands back in mine.

"I didn't know what to do, Adam. I was so used to playing this role, and I had no way to know how anyone would react if I stepped away from that."

We drink our wine in silence, both unsure how to proceed. I don't want to blame her for making the choice she thought was right, but that she worried about coming out to me kinda stings. Plus she acted like the Romantic Terminator this whole time! I felt like I had a target on my back and she didn't even want me. *Whatever. That's* so *not the point right now.*

"OK. First off, thanks for telling me. I hope now we can be friends without all that other stuff." She nods eagerly. Whatever her reasons for keeping this from everyone were, she seems relieved. "Second, why now? Did all the wedding stuff make you just lose it or something?"

She grins mischievously. "It was actually that hottie from the engagement party. The one who brought the champagne flutes?" I choke on my wine, spilling all down my shirt.

"Maya?! You have a thing for *Maya*?!" Emily giggles behind her hands, her shoulders finally relaxing.

"Is that her name? All I knew was that when I looked at her, the way she was swishing around in that pleated skirt..." Emily lets out a wistful sigh. "There was no way I was straight."

Oh my God! She doesn't know the half of it. I laugh so hard, my stomach starts to hurt. All this time she's been hitting on me, and now we want the same woman?! There's a knock at the door and I go to answer it, still chuckling.

At this hour, it's probably a neighbor who needs something. I yank the door open without thinking, without checking the peephole.

But it's not a neighbor. It's not a delivery guy. It's not some kid playing "ding dong, ditch".

Instead, it's Maya standing on the landing, her mouth open in horror. She sees Emily on my couch, hair down. She sees wine and two empty wine glasses. She sees all her insecurities come to life and, judging by her expression, she's jumping to all the absolute wrong conclusions. *Shit!!!!!*

Doing her best to hide the hurt on her face, Maya takes off down the stairs and I leave a confused Emily alone in my apartment to run after her. I catch her by the hand right outside the building before she can break into a run.

"Maya, stop! What you saw is not what you think it was!" This is now twice in one night that we're arguing on the side-walk and I feel a migraine coming on.

I will *not* be branded a cheater. When it comes to women, I never lie and I never cheat; I don't see the point. She tries to pull her hand away, but I hold tight.

"Let me go, Adam!"

"No! Not until you talk to me." She's angry now, nostrils flaring.

"Ok, Adam. Let's talk." Her voice has gone eerily calm. She wipes the tears that threaten to spill with the back of her hand. "Let's talk about how I came over to apologize for doubting your feelings for me earlier only to find you getting cozy with the chick from Cape Cod. Don't think I didn't recognize her." I rake a hand through my hair, beyond frustrated.

"Babe! Seriously. Emily just came to talk! She's going through a tough time and she's my best friend's little sister." I can hear it, the desperation in my voice. Maya simply scoffs.

"Oh yeah. She just came over to talk. At 10pm. With wine!" She narrows her eyes and faces me. "Is that the kind of woman you really want? Is she someone you can show off to your boss?" Tears are streaming down her face and she's no longer trying to hide her hurt from earlier.

It may have only been a couple of months, but I thought I'd earned her trust. Hell, I stood by her when Candy came sniffing around, and it would have been so easy to fall back into that bad habit. I narrow my eyes right back at her.

"Those were *Cory's* words; not mine! If you want me to go and set him straight right now, I'll do it." If he wants to be a dick, so be it. I've still got three other brothers.

She just rolls her eyes and I'm at a loss for words. Nothing I say seems to be getting through to her.

"I don't know what to do, Maya. I want to be with you…"
Her eyes widen. I can't believe it's come to this.

"But I don't know if I can keep going this way. You're beautiful," I sigh. "And I think you know me well enough to know that I don't want to be with Emily, despite what you think you saw. But I can't seem to win against the bullshit you've got in your head. No one else can change how you feel about *you*." I'm tearing up now too. *Dammit.* Thank God my brothers aren't here to see me act like such a simp. I let go of her hand. She's just as shocked as I am by my words.

"Adam? Are you…are you saying it's over?" God, I don't want it to be over. I love her.

My heart gives a painful squeeze at the realization. Yup. I love her. And I already know I want to be with her forever…but not like this. She's got to love herself too. The fact that she doesn't makes my heart hurt even more.

"I'm saying you shouldn't be punishing me for something my idiot brother said. And no one can erase all the bad things you tell yourself." I stop talking to avoid openly crying in front of her. This hurts like hell.

I turn and walk back to my apartment, leaving her staring after me on the street.

CHAPTER TWENTY-EIGHT

Maya

Kiki, a 12-year-old Latina with pigtails and an affinity for stickers and grape chewing gum, jumps up from the table she shares with two older boys and pulls on my protective smock. Even though it's only part-time, I made the smock especially for this program and, because it's what I do, I personalized it. "Ms. Maya. Art Teacher and Professional Weirdo" is stitched on the top corner in red thread. The kids got a kick out of it the first weekend I came. Kiki's expression packs the annoyance of a woman twice her age and she smacks her grape gum for emphasis.

"Ms. Maya! Jeremy's hogging all the beads! I'm trying to finish the necklace I'm making for my mom and he's just gluing them to his janky ass poster board!" I press my lips together to stifle a smile. Are kids still saying "janky"? Miles, a lanky 14-year-old Black kid with glasses looks personally attacked.

"It's not just a poster board, Ms. Maya. It's a *collage.*" Miles actually pulls Kiki's pigtail and she shrieks in surprise. "Besides, we all know Kiki's mom is still in rehab!" A chorus of "oohs" lets me know that the whole class was unfortunately listening in to the conversation. Kiki turns red with rage and throws her unfinished necklace to the ground. What is it with junior high kids that makes them such terrors?

I shoot a death stare to Miles to let him know I'll deal with him later before running after Kiki. She's crying quietly in the empty classroom across the hall and quickly wipes her eyes with her sleeves when I enter. We're in the music room, surrounded by music stands and a few chairs left behind by the jazz band that finished earlier. I pull up a chair next to her.

"It's a lie, Ms. Maya!" she shouts at me defensively. "My mom isn't in rehab; she's in therapy. The necklace is to make her feel better when she comes home." Before I started, Tiffany clued me in on some of the kids in the program. Many came from difficult home situations or were struggling in school; art was to be their outlet to redirect the big feelings hitting kids their age. In Kiki's case, her mom had to be hospitalized for some pretty serious postpartum depression after her baby sister was born. Before the program, she was acting out so much in class, she was in danger of expulsion.

"I know, Kiki." I pat her on the back and try to keep the pity out of my face; these kids hate that. "Your mom just needed a little help to get better. We all do. It's nothing to be ashamed of." Kiki looks at me with red-rimmed eyes shining with tears.

"I hate him, Ms. Maya! He's always trying to put me down in front of everyone!" A part of me wants to commiserate, since what Miles said was vile. If I were her age, Miles may have received a kick to the balls for making fun of my mom. Unfortunately, I have to be the adult in this situation.

"Don't bother hating him, Kiki. He's not worth it." She sniffs again, her tears starting to slow. "Just know that we all have our struggles. It's OK to get help." I smile conspiratorially before adding, "Your necklace will be way better than his collage anyway."

She laughs at that, and wipes her face again. It seems like being an art teacher also means being a therapist. Strangely enough, I actually like it. Maybe some of these kids will learn how to express themselves instead of just lashing out.

"Now let's wipe those tears so you can come back and finish your present." Kiki nods quietly, the puffiness in her eyes already subsiding. "I'll be happy to help you finish it; I love handcrafted jewelry and I'm sure your mom will too."

"Thanks, Ms. Maya." She gives me a shy smile and we both stand to head back to the classroom. When I look up, Tiffany is leaning against the jamb.

"Go ahead, Kiki," Tiffany says. "I'm going to have a word with Ms. Maya."

I try not to look guilty. Shit. Did I handle that wrong?

"Hey, Tiff," I try to keep my tone light. "What's up?" She pulls up a chair and beckons me to sit down.

"I just wanted to have a chat with you real quick." She gestures across the hall. "Don't worry about your class; I called one of the girls from reception to cover for a few minutes so we could talk." The dread builds in my stomach.

"Ok...Is everything OK?" Tiffany looks at me like a third eye just popped up on my forehead.

"Ok? Things are *way* better than OK. I wanted to talk with you to see if...you might be open to staying on with the program when the school year starts."

I sag with relief against a chair that hardly feels sturdy enough for a full-grown adult. *Way to bury the lead, Tiff!*

"Oh my god, Tiffany! Seriously?! Yes, I'd love to." Now it's Tiffany's turn to look relieved. Her smile gets wider and she embraces me in a warm hug.

"I'm so glad to hear it, girl. It's still part time, but it would be after school, from 3 – 6pm Monday through Friday. Then it turns back into a weekend class over all breaks. The hourly pay would still be the same, but I figured that would be OK given you have *It's Personal* too." I swat her arm like the idea of paying me is ridiculous.

"That's totally fine, Tiffany. Thanks so much! I could always use the extra income, and I've actually grown to love these kids since I joined the program. But what happened to what's-her-name that I'm filling in for? Wasn't she supposed to be coming back from her honeymoon?" Tiffany gives me a rueful smile.

"She *was*, but she and her wife fell in love with Spain and decided to extend their trip by another two months. She understood I couldn't start the school year with no art teacher. Plus, the kids love you. Someone comes into my office to sing your praises every week."

I beam with pride. I can't believe a favor to a friend turned into such a great opportunity. It seems my personal life had to go up in flames for my professional life to take off. I wish I could celebrate with Adam...or Denise. Tiffany senses a shift in my mood and puts her hand on my shoulder.

"What is it, Maya? You've seemed a bit down lately." I sigh, worried her comforting words are going to make me crack when I've been working so hard to keep it all together. How ironic would it be if I came in to help a crying student and ended up crying myself?

"It's just...Adam and I had a big fight and essentially broke up. He basically said he couldn't keep convincing me he's really into me if I refuse to believe him." Tears well up in my eyes and I blink them away. Tiffany waits for me to continue, sensing I have more to get off my chest.

"And Denise..." More blinking. "Denise got pissed and took Adam's side. She said I only see the worst in myself, and I just use my friends like therapists when really I need to talk to a professional about my self esteem issues."

And suddenly, it hits me: Denise is right. She said I just dump on my friends and I am *literally* dumping my problems onto another friend, on the verge of tears. And I told her about my fight with Adam, but not that I caught him cozying up with "Ms. Plan B". Deep down, I know there's more than what I saw. What I *think* I saw. The more I think about it, the more I wonder if I made a mistake in not hearing him out. He is clearly crazy about me...and the feeling is mutual. Tiffany lets out a long sigh, resigned.

"Maya," she begins carefully. "You are my girl. You have been since junior high. But you *do* have a tendency to see the worst in yourself. It's like you internalized everything in that stupid slam book years ago and never got past it." Little does she know I think about that book fairly often. Those hurtful words have stuck with me all this time.

"You went to a great school. You spend time doing what you love. You just got *another* job helping kids who need it most, which means not only are you successful, but you're a good person. And whether or not you want to believe it, you're a beautiful woman." I suppress a snort, but she still hears it.

"It's true, Maya. Carrying around a little extra weight doesn't make you ugly. Look at me! I'm thick and got the fellas lining up around the block for a taste!" She preens and clicks her tongue, like the confident queen she's always been.

"You're beautiful, you're amazing, and you've got amazing friends. Own that shit! And then go get your man back." She gives me another hug. "But before you do, go make up with Denise. I'm loving being the three amigas, and it won't work if y'all stay mad at each other."

She gets up to leave and I head back to my classroom. Denise's brutal honesty truly hurt, but it isn't enough to throw away sisterhood.

Back in my place after a sad solo meal at Chipotle where I ate a burrito way too fast to be ladylike, I drop my keys on the kitchen counter. Kiki finished her necklace and Miles got a verbal warning: cut that shit out or make other plans for Saturdays the rest of the summer. Considering he has to be in the program because his dad works two jobs and can't afford a babysitter, Miles swore he'd apologize to Kiki and get his act together. He didn't have to say, but I can tell the whole reason for the incident was that he has a crush on her. I guess teenage boys will forever be clueless when it comes to getting a girl's attention.

I pick up my phone and pet Khan absently while it rings. He purrs like a motorcycle; his way of offering moral support. I'm going to need it. Denise picks up on the third ring.

"Hello?" She doesn't sound pleased to get my call. Maybe this was a bad idea.

"Hi Denise...Do you have a second to talk?" I'm going to do my best not to drop all my problems at her feet anymore.

"I picked up, didn't I?" *Ouch!* Her voice is still full of anger and hurt. *I can do this.*

"I—" I clear my throat, which has suddenly become sandpaper. "I wanted to call and apologize." I hear her sharp intake of breath. She wasn't expecting an apology.

"You were right; I make my problems your problems, and I don't listen as much as I should."

"I may have been right, but I was a bitch." In seconds, the anger has completely drained from her voice. "I didn't have to unload on you like that. You'd just had a crazy stressful night with your boyfriend's family and I made the whole thing about our bullshit." My heart squeezes when I remember all the painful things she yelled.

"Maybe next time, don't wait years to tell me the truth." That's what hurts the most; not only did she think I was a terrible friend, but she waited *years* to tell me anything about it! But if I don't let that go, I'm letting go of a friend that's like a sister. That's major for an only child. "The only reason I always came to you, is because I trust your opinion more than my own. And I always assumed you would do the same if you needed to talk to me about something." I wipe the tears starting to form in my eyes and hear her long exhale over the phone.

"I definitely do, Maya. But I talk to a professional about the really heavy stuff." My shoulders tense as soon as I hear the word "professional". Does she think I'm crazy or something? She must've guessed what my silence is about.

"Don't be like that, Maya. I go, maybe once a month, or more if I'm really going through something. Most of the time, it's like an emotional tune-up to make sure I'm not picking up some unhealthy coping mechanisms. Like excessive retail therapy, or going on a bunch of Tinder hook-ups where I barely remember their name."

I don't know what to say. I didn't realize Denise went to therapy. I didn't realize she had a reason to *need* therapy, though I guess that sounds crazy when I really think about it. I've waited too long to talk again and Denise chuckles.

"All right, all right. Enough of the after school special. What happened with all the Adam stuff? Did y'all make up?" *Ha!* Not exactly.

"We actually kinda...broke up." Denise gasps dramatically.

"Maya! Oh my God. Are you OK? What happened?"

And for the second time today, I tell someone other than Khan all the gory details about the breakup. I even tell her about sneaking into Adam's apartment building to apologize, catching him with Emily and a bottle of wine, and the embarrassing scene on the sidewalk. But it doesn't feel good to get it all off my chest. It feels final, like saying it out loud validates the breakup, and I've been desperate to believe it was all a horrible nightmare.

"Damn, Maya. I'm so sorry," she almost whispers. So was I. "I know you really liked him, even though it'd only been a few months."

"To be honest, I was in love with him. I *am* in love with him." She stifles a snort that would really piss me off if I weren't already devastated.

"How can you be sure? It's hardly been any time at all." Even so, I've known for weeks. I allowed myself to believe it was mutual; that it was just a matter of time before we exchanged the words.

"I just know. That's why I kept running away so much at first. Feeling so strong so fast scared the shit out of me." I hang my head, beyond hopeless. "And now it's over."

"Maya, what the fuck?" My head pops up, shocked at her response. Maybe she's still pissed at me. "You're gonna through away a great guy, a guy you claim to *love*, over one bad fight?"

"But he said he didn't want to see me!"

"No he didn't, bitch!" She's talking to me like I sometimes hear some of the other teachers talk to students. Like she's disappointed I'm not seeing something right in front of me. "He said he's tired of you taking out your insecurities on him when he's clearly crazy about you. I don't believe he was hooking up with Emily for *a minute*. You said he practically had to get a restraining order."

"Oh, I know that," I say absentmindedly. The bombshell that Adam didn't dump me is still swirling around my head, making all other thought almost impossible. *He didn't break up with me?*

"Well, then why haven't you called him? Or texted? Or tried going over there again?" From the sound of it, Denise is gesticulating as she gets more and more hyped.

"I've tried texting and calling," I shrug, defeated. "He doesn't answer my calls, and texts are just, like, one-word answers. He's not trying to link up to talk. He's not trying to see me at all." *And it's excruciating.*

"Oh. Well…Maybe just give it time. Give him time to cool down." She hesitates. "And…maybe give yourself time to talk to someone to help with your emotional stuff. There's nothing wrong with it. Just think about it."

I had never thought about therapy, but Denise is my girl, and she wouldn't suggest it if it weren't legit. Plus, she seems like the most confident, bold woman I know, next to Tiffany. Maybe it's because of therapy. Maybe it's time to let some of my baggage go.

CHAPTER TWENTY-NINE

Adam

"Whattup, bro?! To what do I owe the surprise visit?" Bryan answers the door wearing just boxers, looking sweaty and out of breath. I hear D'Angelo playing from the other room. *Jesus!* Why would you answer the door in the middle of having sex with your fiancee?!

"Oh, I caught you in the middle of something," I mutter as I back away from the apartment door. "I'll call you and we'll grab lunch." Bryan looks at me like I'm being ridiculous and literally laughs in my face. Though he looks like an Abercrombie Chad, he's always had a warm, friendly laugh.

"Shut the fuck up, man. We were just..." he looks to his bedroom, chagrined. "...finishing up." Oh my God.

"Hiiiii, Adam!" Jessi calls from the other room. "You've got terrible timing!" Her words are harsh, but I can hear the laughter in her voice. Bryan is chuckling to himself.

"I'm a lucky man. What can I say?" I smile in response to my friend's lovestruck mood. If only I were so lucky...I definitely wouldn't leave making love with Maya to answer the fucking door, though.

"Yeah, well..." I rock back and forth on my feet, unsure how to broach the subject. "Do you have a sec? I need to talk to you about something."

Sensing the seriousness of my tone, he pulls me the rest of the way into the apartment and shuts the door behind us. He grabs a seat on the sofa and pats the seat next to him. As I approach, I see his dick winking at me through the hole in his boxers and immediately look at the ceiling.

"Uh..." I clear my through. "Dude...Uh, your boxers..." I keep my eyes trained on the ceiling for longer than necessary, not trusting Bryan not to trick me into looking at his balls or something. White dudes are crazy like that.

"C'mon, Adam. You can sit down. I'm not gonna make you look at my dick when you really need to talk." I take a seat next to him and shove my hands in the pockets of my jeans. Bryan and I don't really do this; if I want to talk about something real, I usually go to my brothers. But with Cory gunning for the role of "World's Biggest Douchebag"...

"So...I came to talk to you about a girl." Bryan grabs me in a bro-hug, excited for some unknown reason.

"Adam! Oh shit! *Finally.*" He leans over to me, conspiratorially. "Jessi thought you were gonna go the George Clooney route, but I knew it wouldn't be long before some woman finally caught your eye." He leans back and yells in the direction of the bedroom.

"Babe! You owe me one killer back rub! Adam's got a girlfriend." Jessi opens the door and leans against the jamb.

"No shit?" Bryan nods and grins. "Damn. There goes Emily's wedding weekend sex." Bryan's smile slides off his face and Jessi laughs before closing the door behind her. Bryan's still facing the door, frowning.

"Babe! You weren't really trying to hook up Adam and my little sis, were you?" He's met with silence. "Babe?!"

If only they both knew, but Emily's secret is not mine to tell. I clear my throat and Bryan begrudgingly turns around.

"You wouldn't really have slept with Em, would you?" I do my best impression of appalled.

"Of course not, bro. That's your little sister. Now can we please get back to *my* problem?" Bryan relaxes and gives me his full attention.

"Sorry, man. What's up?" I take a deep breath, unsure of where to begin.

"Well, like I was starting to say, I'm seeing someone. I've been seeing her since your engagement party actually." Bryan perks up.

"My engagement party. Shit, do I know her?"

"Nah, man. She's the one who made those custom champagne flutes." Bryan nods and indicates I should continue my story.

"Anyway, things have been going well. Really well. *Scary* well, even. So well that I brought her to Sunday dinner with my family. Bryan claps a hand on my shoulder, so hard I briefly lose my breath.

"That's major, Adam! So what's up? Am I gonna be going to *your* wedding next? Are you asking me to be your best man?" He turns around again. "Hey babe!" he yells again. I quickly grab his arm and shush him.

"Cool it, man! No wedding bells for me yet." Despite my panicked expression, Bryan just smirks.

"You may carry on, but don't think I didn't hear the 'yet'." I sigh and continue.

"Well, Mom and Dad love Maya. Like Mom already wants her to move in. But Cory said some really shitty things about her. I'm not sure what his deal is. And she walked in on him being a jerk and then we had a huge fight."

"Oh man. I'm sorry, Adam." He pats my shoulder again, this time without the bodily injury. "It's no big deal, though. I know you're a newbie to the whole dating thing, but real couples fight." I give him a small smile.

"I know, man. You're totally right. And I was all set to make up with her. I called her a bunch of times." Bryan interrupts to make the whipped sound, accompanied by the juvenile hand gesture. *What are we, sixteen?* "But when she finally came over to make up, another woman was there and she got the wrong idea." Bryan rakes his hand through his hair.

"Another woman? Dude? What were you thinking?" I clench my fists by my side and use all my willpower not to rat out Emily.

"I was thinking," I say between clenched teeth, "that my friend needed a shoulder to cry on and it was the right thing to do. Nothing happened. It wasn't a date or anything like that."

"Is that how your girl sees it?" Bryan asks, doubt etched into his face. My shoulders slump.

"No. Of course not. She was pissed. She finally called me back the other day and we've been texting a little, but....I'm not sure I'm cut out for this." Bryan shakes his head.

"Cut out for what? Dating?" He chuckles to himself and I feel myself getting defensive.

"Well...Yeah. Hooking up is so much easier than this." At that, Bryan has the nerve to roll his eyes. This is exactly why I prefer to talk to my brothers.

"Look, Adam," he says, with a stern tone I've never heard from him. "I'm not some dating guru. Jessi and I are getting married just as much because she's forgiven me for my bonehead moves as because I swept her off her feet. But if what you have together is real, it's worth these little hiccups." I'm too stunned by Bryan's speech to respond and he pats my back.

"Do you love her?" That is the question, isn't it? Because if I *love* her, then this isn't over. It can't be. I shrug, still not ready to admit my feelings for Maya.

"I don't know." Bryan sighs.

"I suggest you figure that out. Then you'll know what your next move is." We sit in silence as I mull over his words.

"Thanks for the talk, man. I know it's weird, us talking about this girl stuff, but I really appreciate it."

"Not as weird as this," he says, nudging me with his elbow. I look down to see him holding both his balls in a clenched fist. I punch him in the shoulder and jump up off the couch.

"Gross, dude. That's my cue to leave," I say over my shoulder on the way to the door. He's still laughing as the door closes behind me. What a dick.

Thankfully the wedding stuff is about to be done. It's just a little over a month until the big day. Bryan may be a bit of a douche sometimes, but I'm really happy for him. He and Jessi are obviously in love. I know the feeling.

Ugh. Things between Maya and I are...weird. I think I love her, but I don't really know how things are gonna go. I don't know if we can get past the bullshit with my brother and the bullshit with Emily, and just be together. She might just run away. Am I still willing to chase her after all this drama?

CHAPTER THIRTY

Maya

I had to park six blocks from my apartment, but I don't mind. There's a cool breeze and it smells like someone is burning leaves nearby. Fall in New York is my favorite, hands down. The humidity lets up, the leaves start to change, and I can finally wear all my sweaters without getting weird looks. Adam never minded my sweaters, but...

I pick up the pace and turn the music in my earbuds up louder to clear that unpleasant thought. It's been three weeks since Damon's going-away dinner...and the huge fight afterward. Adam's been answering my texts but it's...different. He's closed off and distant. He doesn't call anymore. He doesn't answer when I try to call. And we haven't seen each other since that night. I've showed up a few times, but I never get past the buzzer. Despite Denise's hopes,—and mine—the weird, crazy, amazing, spectacular, *fantastic* thing I had going with Adam seems like it's over for good.

Once I got home that horrible night and wasn't seeing red, I knew I was to blame. Emily is a skank and I hope she trips down a flight of stairs, but I shouldn't have jumped to conclusions about what happened. I should've listened when Adam tried to explain. Even if she *was* hitting on him, can I really blame him for that? I mean, he *is* super hot. And he was right. I *did* know him well enough to know he didn't want to be with her.

With the pause between Adam and I, I've been killing it at work. I'm still glowing with the thought of continuing to teach my Summer kids when school starts. And I'm so relieved Denise and I made up. It hurt, and we both made mistakes, but I think I made more of them.

Also with the help of the pause, I can appreciate exactly how much my friends are here for me when I need them. After the last time I tried to see Adam (unsuccessfully), I went to Tiffany's and we belted out Kelly Clarkson and Cardi B for hours at the karaoke bar down the block. It beats crying. Then once D and I were back on good terms, the girls and I did a movie marathon (no romance movies allowed), and another boozy brunch.

I drop my bag, keys, and a box of art supplies right inside the door of my apartment. Khan greets me with head butts—he's always happy to see me, or at least he pretends to be because I feed him daily. I give him a rueful smile as he winds figure eights around my legs. I nearly wipe out, and my cell phone flies from

the pocket of my oversized sweater. When I pick it up to put it
on the counter, Adam's texts are like a slap in the face.

Adam

Are you sure you can't come over?

Adam: I want to. Just don't think it
would be a good idea.

I absently pet Khan. He's purring loud enough to drown out
a sewing machine. At least *someone* is feeling good right now.
I prepare Khan's wet food and put the kettle on. Maybe some
chamomile will soothe my nerves. Khan dives face first into his
bowl, completely forgetting me. Let's hope that's not a trait
shared by all males.

It's almost killed me not to see Adam, to feel him, not to
get a chance to apologize...because he was right about me. Just
because Cory managed to voice all my insecurities, didn't mean
Adam felt the same way. Adam's words and actions never said
anything but that he loved being with me, and loved making
love to me. Sure, he hadn't said those three words that were
always on the tip of my tongue when we were together, but that
didn't mean he was faking anything with me. From the moment
I met him, he seemed genuine. He wasn't afraid to say he was
interested, he wasn't afraid to be seen with me in public, and he
wasn't afraid to show his affection...sometimes three times in a ni
ght.

My cheeks turn pink and I try to get my mind out of the gutter. Things might be over between us, but Ms. Kitty downstairs has *not* gotten the memo! Practically every night since *that* night, I've woken up with my hand inside my panties. The sex isn't the only reason I'm in love with Adam, but damn if it doesn't help a lot!

The whistle from the kettle breaks into my thoughts and I scroll to his texts from a week after the fight.

Adam

Adam: FYI: I talked to Cory.

You did?

Adam: He's really sorry about what he said. When I talked to him, he said he'd already talked to Mom and Dad about what a dick he was at dinner.

I appreciate the apology, but you didn't have to fight with your brother on my account.

Adam: Yes I did. He was out of line.

Did you maybe want to come over and talk? No pressure.

Adam: Can't tonight.

Oh, OK.

I set the tea on the counter to brew and fail miserably at not thinking about Adam. Thank God I've already got an appointment with Dr. Jamison tomorrow morning. I know what I'd like to talk about, but my guess is that she's going to grill me on my parents, asking me to make a dream journal, or some other bullshit. I'm not too happy about tomorrow's session, but Denise is right—something's gotta give, and my girls aren't professionals.

"So, Maya. What brings you here today?" The office has art pieces from a well-traveled life, including masks from Mali and terra cotta pots from the hills of New Mexico. Denise told me she trusts Dr. Jamison implicitly. She certainly has great taste. The leather of the butter-soft couch couldn't be anything but Italian. I rub my palms on it before raising my eyes to meet Dr. Jamison's.

"I've kinda got...Self-esteem issues." I look at my hands again before continuing. "I've never had trouble dating decent men, but, in my head, none of them are really interested...At least, not because of my looks." Dr. Jamison purses her lips and pushes her glasses up the bridge of her nose.

"OK. Did something in particular happen that caused you to seek therapy now?" *Busted.*

"I was seeing someone pretty great. His brother said some not nice things about me. And I took it out on my boyfriend." She starts taking notes and I rush to elaborate.

"It wasn't just that, though. I've felt this way for a while. I used to be teased about it growing up and, even though I'm grown and I'm successful, those bad thoughts have stayed inside me and come out whenever I try on a swimsuit, or start dating someone new, or look at movies and magazines with their unfair beauty standards." Dr. Jamison puts her pen down and folds her hands in her lap.

"I'm sorry you're going through all of that, Maya. Feelings of unworthiness are a common reason for people to seek therapy." She smiles warmly at me, and I immediately start to relax. I can see why Denise likes her.

"Would it surprise you to know that, despite those unfair beauty standards you mentioned, people are three times more likely to search for pornography featuring a plus size woman over a thin one?" My eyes widen and I almost drop my purse on the floor. Dr. Jamison chuckles at my embarrassment.

"Pornography is nothing to be ashamed of, Maya. We can even talk about it in our sessions, if you'd like." I secure my purse more closely in my lap and shake my head nervously. "Fine. But my point is, these sessions are for your benefit. You don't have to shy away from more mature or even taboo topics." She picks back up her pen and notepad.

"Feelings of inadequacy despite external circumstances that contradict those feelings are usually caused by some traumatic incident." She levels her gaze at me and pushes her glasses up the bridge of her nose. "Can you recall an incident, maybe in adolescence, when you were, perhaps, bullied for your size or physical characteristics?"

Without hesitation, the insults come into sniper-like focus.

"Ms. Nappy Head"

"Thunder thighs!"

"Try Jenny Craig!"

"Call me when you lose 50 pounds!"

My palms start to sweat and I look up to see Dr. Jamison has noticed. I avert my eyes again. How pathetic that I have to go to a therapist to work out some junior high shit. Am I seriously not past this? I snort, almost disgusted with my emotional immaturity. Dr. Jamison's gaze sharpen.

"What's that? What were you thinking just then?" Is this woman psychic?

"I...," I start, hesitant to be truly open with her. What the heck; she said to be honest. "I was thinking how pathetic it is that I'm hung up on bullshit from junior high." She raises an eyebrow in question. "There was a slam book. Some bullshit like in 'Mean Girls', except the book was passed around for everyone to write in. It was basically a way to talk shit and to see how people really felt about you." Dr. Jamison didn't look impressed.

"They called me names. Things like 'fatty' and 'nappy head'." I keep my eyes trained on my hands folded in my lap. "Then the head mean girl embarrassed me right in front of my crush...Well, in front of, like, the whole school." I look up to see her irritated expression. Is she irritated because my problems are a waste of her time?

"What's pathetic is how unoriginal the kids at your school were when it came to insulting you. Did you know, Maya, that the slam book goes as far back as the 1920s? A century's passed and still no one has come up with a better outlet for teenage angst." I smile at Dr. Jamison. She's a one-woman trivia machine. Despite her radical candor, I get a good vibe from her.

"Over the next few sessions, we're going to peel back the layers and see what might be at the core of these feelings of inadequacy. Then we will work to build your belief in yourself, so you don't rely so heavily on external sources of validation." She returns my smile, and I'm feeling lighter already. I should've started therapy a long time ago.

"Thank you, Dr. Jamison."

CHAPTER THIRTY-ONE

Adam

I can barely hear myself think in this place and the lights are starting to give me a migraine. Bryan wanted his bachelor party to be like something out of "The Hangover", so we are in Vegas – of course – and sitting in the third bar of the night. This one comes with strippers, a mechanical bull, and even an all-you-can-eat buffet. But, who wants to eat at a strip club? Yuck.

Bryan is across the room having the time of his life with one woman giving him a lap dance while another pours tequila down his throat. Knowing how he was in college, I sometimes still can't believe he's giving it all up to get married. Jessi's great and they're great together, but his little black book was almost as big as mine.

I got a handwritten card from Emily a couple days after *that night*. She apologized again for being "overly persistent" and swore to respect my boundaries going forward. She also apologized for being there when another woman came over, though I don't think she recognized it was Maya. She just saw me slamming the door in her face when I ran after someone, and then she left without a word when I came back looking like I'd been hit by a truck...emotionally, at least. God, that night sucked. We've only been speaking via email lately, just to be safe.

With that issue essentially handled, I had to talk to my brother. Cory had been a complete ass and he knew it. I was finally calm enough to call him a week after the dinner. He answered after the second ring.

"If you're calling to say I was an asshole, Mom and Dad already beat you to it." *Alright, Mom and Dad!* They hated to make a scene in front of company, but I knew they noticed how Cory was behaving.

"Good. Since when do any of us have a say in who the other is dating?!" I yell. Never in a million years would I have pulled that shit on any of my brothers. Bro code says that you wait until the woman isn't around to stage any needed interventions about a problematic relationship. Lucky me; I'm the first one to have to enforce it. Cory sighs.

"I fucked up, bro. The market was down that day and I lashed out. She's not *my* type, but she seems perfectly nice."

"I don't give a fuck if she's not your type! She *my* girlfriend, and she was there because I *asked* her to be. Because I'm *serious* about Maya!" I didn't realize how mad I still was at Cory until I was yelling at him. Knowing he was in the wrong, he doesn't try to interrupt.

"How serious are we talking, bro?" he asks quietly. I can't believe this asshole has the nerve to question me.

"I don't know...Serious!" Cory looks at me doubtfully and I shout back, "*Really* serious!" Not my finest argument. I may need to tell the truth, the whole truth, and nothing but the truth to make Cory understand. I release a breath I didn't realize I was holding.

"I love her. Like, *really* love her. I haven't bought a ring or anything," I hear Cory gasp over the phone. "But I think I might buy her a ring eventually. Assuming we get back together." For a while, there's just silence from Cory's side of the line. Then—

"Damn. Adam! Why didn't you let me know it was so serious? Maya could be my *sister* some day?!" I smile at that thought. Things are tough now, but Maya in my bed, by my side, with my family? It all sounds amazing. I lower my hackles slightly since he actually sounds sincere.

"I assumed it was obvious when I brought her to meet Mom, Dad, and all my asshole brothers," I say, my voice dripping with sarcasm. I suppose Cory has no frame of reference, since I've never brought a woman home before. Before Maya, I never let a woman stay over; now I'm contemplating forever with a woman I've known less than three months. Not that I care, but that's not exactly the norm. Cory clears his throat, sounding embarrassed even over the phone.

"Again…I'm sorry, bro. I'll be sure to apologize in person at Mom & Dad's party, OK?" Assuming she's there…

"Well…Don't let it happen again. I plan to be with Maya long-term, and I don't need any of your so-called helpful comments."

"Understood."

Even though I've patched things up with Cory, I'm still not ready to face Maya. If I'm being honest, it hurts that she doesn't already know how I feel about her, that she doesn't trust me. I haven't stopped texting her, though; I can't go cold turkey when it comes to that woman. But I've kept my distance, and I know she's noticed.

I take another sip of my Jack & Coke and try to shake my gloomy thoughts. A tall brunette with fake boobs wearing nothing but a g-string and pasties practically slithers into my lap and bats her eyelash extensions at me.

"Hey, big boy. Why so glum?" She gyrates in my lap as she speaks. She looks like one of the countless women I wasted time with before Maya.

"No reason. Just taking a break from the bachelor party festivities." I nod my head towards Bryan and she giggles.

"Oh, I see." She grinds even harder on my lap, probably thinking she's found her marks for the night. "Well, if you boys are looking to take this party to the next level, me and a few other girls can come to your room and turn that frown upside down." She winks for emphasis and I turn away to hide my cringe.

What the hell am I doing here? I've never had any trouble getting a woman into her birthday suit, and the women in here have one goal: separate you from as much of your cash as possible by any means necessary. I'm not dumb enough or drunk enough to invite one to my room. Especially not when only one woman is worth my attention, and I'm the idiot keeping her at arms length.

I politely excuse myself and walk over to let Bryan know I have a headache—which is true, despite the hard time the guys try to give me. They're so blasted on whiskey and Dos Equis®, they can hardly stand. No way they make it through Bryan's "Hangover"-themed bar crawl at this rate. I push my way out of the club and head back to the hotel.

Thirty minutes later, I've showered, taken two Excedrin, and ordered room service to soak up the liquor currently giving me the spins. I sit on the edge of the bed and grab my cell. I might be a bit drunk, but this call can't wait. After four rings, I hear her sleep-scratchy voice on the line.

"...Mmm. Hello?" Damn. She sounds half asleep. Maybe I shouldn't have called at – I look at my watch – one in the morning. I totally forgot about time zones.

"Oh shoot. I didn't mean to wake you, Maya." I hear a gasp and then fumbling, like she almost dropped the phone.

"Adam! Uh, no, no. It's fine. I just fell asleep on the couch. What's up?"

"I know it's been a minute...I just had to hear your voice." I hear her sigh and my chest immediately tightens.

"You could have talked to me when I called before." I can hear the hurt in her voice. Hurt that I put there.

"I know, babe. I'm sorry. I just needed some time to sort things out." God, I sound like such a jerk.

"And have you?" she whispers. "Have you sorted things out?"

"I have. That's why I had to call...I missed you." I hear her breath catch, but she stays silent.

"Hmmm." She seems pissed. Why wouldn't she be after I basically ghosted her at the first sign of trouble? Maybe I should've begged to get back together in person rather than over the phone in the middle of the night. She interrupts my thoughts before I can spiral into full-blown heartbreak.

"I was actually going to try calling you again. I just wanted you to know I started seeing someone." My heart plummets to my stomach. Of course she was seeing someone! Could I be any more of a bonehead for waiting so long to make up with her? I fail miserably at keeping the disappointment out of my voice.

"Oh really? How long have you been seeing each other?" My migraine graduates from splitting to stabbing and I pinch the bridge of my nose.

"It's only been a couple of weeks, but I feel really good about it." She actually sounds excited about this guy! If I could go back in time and uninvent phones to prevent this conversation, I would.

"Well...I wish you all the best and I hope he makes you happy. Listen, Maya, I gotta get back to–"

"Adam, wait," she interrupts. "The person I'm seeing is a *woman*." That's a surprise. I knew she was open, but–

"Her name is Dr. Jamison. I'm seeing her to work on some of that baggage you mentioned. She's my therapist."

For several moments, I'm too stunned to speak. I hadn't meant to make her feel like she was broken. Now, she's seeing a therapist because of something I said.

"Wow." I nervously clear my throat. "Uh...that's great, Maya."

"Thanks," she says, sounding calm and not at all pissed her boyfriend told her to seek professional help.

"You know...you didn't have to do that just because of what I said," I say quietly. She just laughs.

"I didn't. I did it because my insecurities have been weighing me down for long enough. It's time to see if some professional help can...well, help." She seems more confident even over the phone. I breathe a huge sigh of relief and can't wipe the smile off my face.

"Now I really *am* happy for you. But why did you do that! You knew what it sounded like." I hear an evil laugh across the line and wish I were there to give her a proper spanking.

"Maybe it was a little petty, but you hurt my feelings when you didn't answer my calls or come over." Though it hurt like hell, that's fair. She clears her throat and her voice is much more somber.

"I'm so sorry for not believing you. I could've handled that whole situation better."

"Babe, I'm sorry, too. I never should've let it go unresolved for so long."

"So…What now?" Her voice drops into a sultry range. "Do you want to come over to make up?" *More than anything!*

"I wish, but I'm stuck in Vegas for Bryan's bachelor party. I'll be back in town tomorrow."

"Oh. OK." Her pouting is literally audible and it forces a laugh from my chest.

"I'll be back tomorrow. You know…I was thinking. Would you like to be my date to the wedding?" My invitation is met with silence and the smile falls from my face.

"Are you sure? Won't it be awkward after the champagne flute incident?" I suppress a laugh. Emily is the only person other than myself who even knows about it, and she might want Maya there more than even me.

"No way. No one will even remember that. And if they do, they can take it up personally with me." *I'll* never forget that day because it brought Maya into my life. She giggles and I can finally breathe again. I don't think I'll ever get enough of her.

"In that case, of course I'll go with you."

We settle into an easy conversation and I fall asleep to the sound of her light snoring.

CHAPTER THIRTY-TWO

Maya

Bryan and Jessi's wedding is the epitome of "gilding the lily". The driveway to the venue is lined with pink and white rose topiaries. Footmen clad in pink and white livery escort each guest down a white velvet carpet into a grand atrium. While waiting under a chandelier big enough for the Waldorf Astoria, I receive the bride and groom's signature cocktail: a French martini. I barely resist rolling my eyes. Even the *cocktail* is pink. I wonder if this Bryan guy had any say in the planning.

I scan the other guests in the foyer and try not to gawk at the majestic surroundings. Thank God Denise helped me get ready, ensuring I was dressed to kill. I had planned to wear a basic black dress and one of my cardigans, but Denise scoffed at that idea when she heard the wedding was in the Hamptons. Instead of the black number, I'm wearing a forest green wrap dress made of crushed velvet with a ruffled skirt. The neckline is off the shoulder, prominently displaying my bountiful cleavage. I've accessorized with rich gold platforms and layered gold necklaces. At Adam's request, I'm wearing my hair up in a bun, my locs curled for a more formal look.

My heart is fluttering with anticipation. Though Adam got back from Vegas a few days ago, his best man duties have kept him too busy to meet up. At least we got to talk on the phone every night. There'd been so much shameless flirting and teasing, a cold shower became part of my bedtime routine. I can't wait to see him. Unfortunately, since he's in the wedding party, I'll have to wait until the reception to get any time alone with him. An usher takes my empty glass, hands me a program fit for a royal wedding, and walks me to my seat at the back of the groom's side.

The inside of the venue is even more luxurious than I expected. The entire ceiling is covered in hanging blossoms, making me feel like I've stumbled into *The Secret Garden*. The colors, of course, are white and pink, and tall, white votives line the center aisle. An actual cherry blossom tree stands at the end of the aisle. Jesus! How rich *are* Bryan and Jessi? I find my seat next to two older women in large hats and brightly colored dresses just as the string quartet begins playing Pachelbel's Canon in D Major.

And there he is.

Adam's wearing a black tuxedo that's expertly tailored to highlight his toned body even beneath his dress shirt and pants. The five o'clock shadow is back, and somehow he's making a pink bowtie and cummerbund look incredibly sexy.

The skank from his apartment that horrible night has her pink talons wrapped around his forearm. *You better get your hands off my man, bitch.* She's politely smiling at the guests, sometimes nodding in silent greeting. Then her eyes lock with mine and go wide with recognition. *That's right, chick!* He chose *me*! I see something in her eyes. Not anger. Not gloating. Something much more...intense. *Interested.* What the hell?

I take a deep breath and focus on how handsome Adam looks instead of the home-wrecker on his arm. Thanks to some new internal mantras from Dr. Jamison,—*I am enough. I am beautiful. I am valued. I deserve what I want.*—she can't ruin my evening, not even with her weird stares.

He walks in time to the music, escorting the maid of honor down the aisle before taking his place at the head of the line of groomsmen. As the flower girls process in, he looks around, obviously searching for someone. At last, our eyes meet and my insides turn to liquid heat at the promise in his gaze. How he feels about me is written all over his face just as it's written on mine: he loves me. There is no doubt.

The ceremony was beautiful, though I felt every second I had to wait to be in Adam's arms. He played the part of supportive best man well: handing Bryan the rings before the vows, and handing him his pocket square when he began to cry. Despite all the pomp and circumstance, Bryan and Jessi appear to truly love each other. From the many weddings I've attended, that's not always the case.

Overflowing with emotion at the ceremony and the love I saw in Adam's eyes, I allow myself to imagine what Adam would be like at our wedding. Would he be strong, or would the magnitude of the day get to him?

At the reception, the newlyweds dance to Ed Sheeran's "Thinking Out Loud" before the DJ opens the floor up to everyone. Adam makes a bee line for me, pulling me out of my seat and onto the dance floor. I overhear a few people murmuring as we dance.

"Who is that woman dancing with the best man?"
"Why isn't she sitting with him at the head table?"
"I didn't know Adam was into women...like that."

Adam seems to hear none of the chatter, staring meaningfully into my eyes. I use the mantras to push aside my worries about what others think of me and simply enjoy the feel of Adam's warm chest against my cheek. *Whether you like it or not, Adam is here with me!*

"You look amazing." His voice raises goosebumps on my arms. I missed him so much!

"Thank you. You don't look half bad yourself." He caresses the skin on the back of my neck and I can't help but shiver.

"This is why I wanted you to wear your hair up. Your neck drives me crazy." His hand continues down my back to clutch my waist. "Among other things."

My voice is stuck in my throat and I can only hum in appreciation. We sway wordlessly as Ed Sheeran sings about his soulmate taking him into her loving arms. As the song ends, Adam moves closer to whisper in my ear.

"We need to talk. Privately." When I nod, he takes my hand and leads me off the dance floor. More stares and murmurs follow us as we make our way through the crowd. The maid of honor is also on the move, making a bee line directly toward us. Jesus, I hope she's not going to make a scene. This is a *wedding*, for God sakes!

She stops abruptly, cornering us between another topiary and a table piled high with petit fours. She stares at our joined hands and looks...bewildered.

"Maya?...You're here?...with *Adam*?" I'm so shocked she knows my name, I forget to be offended at her implication that Adam wouldn't bring his girlfriend with him tonight.

"Yeah," I say, confused. "Where else would I be?"

What's-her-name cuts a sharp glance at Adam, who is unsuccessfully fighting a smile. He gestures towards me.

"Emily, this is my girlfriend, Maya." Emily's jaw drops wide enough to catch flies. "We've been seeing each other ever since the engagement party." I preen a bit at the pride in Adam's voice and give him a small peck on the cheek. If she didn't know he was seeing someone, maybe I can forgive her shooting her shot. Maybe. *Someday.*

She recovers quickly to paste a polite smile on her face. "It's nice to meet you officially, Maya. I hope you enjoy the rest of your evening." Then, just as abruptly as she stopped in front of us, she turns on her heel towards the bar. I look at Adam.

"Uh, what was that?"

He grabs my hand and resumes pulling me towards the hallway for some privacy.

"I'll tell you later."

As soon as we're alone, I push him against the wall and kiss him until we're out of breath. My lipstick is gone, and my hands are clinging to his shirt inside his jacket.

"God damn! That was *some* kiss," he says against my lips. I can tell he's trying to get his breathing under control. I kiss him again, softly this time, kissing down his neck, pushing off his jacket, reaching for his bowtie before his hands come up to stop me

.

"Wait a second. Wait, Maya." He's stopping me, but it's not a rejection. He keeps holding my hands and places a kiss on my fingers.

"I don't want to go any further without letting you know how I feel." He swallows and looks unsure. He's so cute when he's nervous. He looks up and meets my eyes, the uncertainty gone.

"I love you. I love you and I want to be with you as long as you'll have me." I smile at him, my heart fully open, and touch his cheek.

"I love you too, Adam. I think I have for a while now." He lets out a huge sigh of relief and pulls me into his arms, smiling ear to ear.

"Oh my God. That's great news. Because if you didn't love me back I was going to have to go with Plan B." We start swaying gently to the music that seeps through the walls.

"What was Plan B?" He just smiles and shakes his head.

"It doesn't matter. Ever since I met you, you were always my first choice."

Epilogue

ADAM

Two months later...

My mouth waters at the sight of Maya on my bed in that woodland nymph costume. Dainty horns peek out from among her locs, which flow alluringly against her peasant top and corset. I brought her in here as the last stop on a tour of my childhood home,—we didn't make it up here the last time—but seeing her in my room—the same room where I jerked off daily and fantasized nightly, the same room I snuck Melissa Donovan into that day after yearbook committee, and Seana Kingsley after Homecoming—awakens a primal desire to make some new sexual memories right now...with Maya. She turns back from looking at the posters on my walls to see me staring at her like a panther. She raises an eyebrow.

"What are you thinking right now, Adam?" She quirks her mouth into a crooked smile. I lock the door and start moving towards her.

"Oh no. Wait a minute. We are *not* having sex, Adam!" I'm sitting next to her on the bed now, and I put my hand on her thigh.

"Just because you're Pan to my woodland nymph, doesn't mean I agreed to recreate some *forest magic* on the same bed you jerked off in for the first time.

I laugh out load. She's such a perv...but also...*correct*.

"Who said anything about sex?" I ask, trying my best to sound innocent. The horns on my head aren't doing me any favors. I slide my hand higher up her thigh and she giggles.

"Stop it, Adam! I am NOT having sex in your childhood room." She's using her sexy, bossy tone and I know she's waiting for any excuse to crack. I wouldn't mind pretending I snuck her into my room after skipping out on fifth period, hoping my parents don't come home early. I gently nibble her earlobe and feel her whole body shudder. I move my hand up higher still, under her skirt. She shakes her head, but leans back on the bed, unconsciously spreading her legs. I chuckle against her ear.

"Your mouth is saying 'no', but the rest of your body is saying 'yes'." I kiss down her neck into the cleavage her red dress displays beautifully, and squeeze each breast until her nipples are harder than diamonds. A small moan escapes her lips.

"Adam...Mmmm...You know I love it when you," I slip her dress further down and pull one of her nipples into my mouth. "Uhmmm...yeah, *that*. But we can't have sex in your parent's house during a party! What if someone hears us?"

She's breathing heavily now, and I pull her other nipple into my mouth, lightly biting it before soothing it with my tongue. She moans again, this time loud enough for me to really worry about someone hearing us, and I put my hand over her mouth.

"No one will hear us if we're quiet." I keep one hand over her mouth, and move the other under her dress and into her panties. She's soaking wet, like she was thinking about having sex before I even touched her. I tease her clit with my fingertips and she jerks against my palm and moans again. If my hand hadn't been covering her mouth, someone DEFINITELY would have heard us that time.

"Tsk tsk tsk. Maya," I say in a flirty warning. "Do you *want* someone to hear us?" She shakes her head. In her eyes, I can see the fear of getting caught, along with the excitement of fucking me right here and now. She takes my hand off her mouth and pushes me onto my back, straddling my hips.

"I don't know, Adam," she says in her best vixen voice. "I think it might be you who has trouble keeping quiet." To prove her point, she grinds her heat against the ridge of my erection and I groan in pleasure. Her smile is triumphant, and she grinds again, loving the feel of my dick twitching with need against her.

While looking down at me with a wicked grin, she reaches between us to unbuckle my belt and unzip my pants. My dick pushes down the rim of my boxers to land into her hand with a slap. She giggles again.

"Well, *he's* certainly happy to see me." She uses one hand to cup my balls and the other to firmly grip the base of my cock. Her hands are so warm and her grip is so perfect that I moan and stroke uncontrolled into her hand.

"Shhh," she whispers, and lowers herself on top of me to kiss my neck, my collarbone, and down my chest as she nimbly unbuttons my dress shirt. Before all rational thought leaves my head, I remind myself why I brought her up here in the first place. As much as I want to, it wasn't to role-play about the computer geek and the sexy art student. I savor the feeling of her mouth on my chest for a few more seconds before pushing up to a seated position and placing Maya's plump, perfect ass next to me where it's slightly less distracting. She furrows her brow in question and I take both her hands in mine to reassure her.

"Don't worry. Nothing's wrong." I swallow, though my throat suddenly feels dry and my tongue has mysteriously grown three sizes in the last three seconds. *It's all in your head, Adam.* "I just wanted to talk to you about something before I lose my nerve." She squeezes my hands and all playfulness is gone from her eyes.

"OK. I'm listening. What's up?" Her big doe eyes stare into mine and I struggle to maintain my composure. She's just so beautiful.

"When I purchased those champagne flutes," I begin haltingly, "I didn't know they'd lead me to meet such an amazing woman." She smiles warmly at the compliment and I feel more empowered to continue.

"Before you, I had a string of women that were nothing special. I didn't even let women cuddle!" Maya's eyes have gone wide, but she doesn't interrupt. "I didn't know it then, but I was already losing interest in the meaningless hookups. I wanted something real; some*one* real." I avert my eyes, ashamed at my bachelor behavior. Maya continues to stroke my hand.

"I don't feel that way anymore, Maya. I actually feel quite the opposite." God, why am I so nervous? I love her. She says she loves me and I believe her. I take a deep breath to give myself the strength to forge ahead.

"I was wondering...would you...?" My hands start shaking and Maya looks at me with concern. She never lets go of my hands.

"Adam? What is it? You're starting to scare me." *Shit*. I knew I was going to mess this up. I take a deep breath and take Maya by the shoulders so we're facing each other.

"All the time I've spent with you has been amazing. Whether we're playing naked Twister," Maya covers her mouth to stifle a laugh. "Or just ordering breakfast after a night of too many gin & tonics, being with you is incredible. I'm bummed whenever you have to leave to go back to your place, and I hate not waking up to you every morning." Maya's eyes are as wide as saucers. It's now or never. "Maya Davis. I know it's only been a few months, and that you might think I'm crazy, but I already know you're the love of my life...Will you marry me?"

At first, Maya just blinks. I know it's fast, but I was certain we felt the same way about each other. My lower back starts to sweat. Before I consider jumping out of the second floor window, the corners of her mouth lift. It starts as a shy smile and gets wider until she looks like the Cheshire Cat. She jumps back onto me, knocking me over with the force, and kisses all over my lips, cheeks, neck, and then back up again. This seems promising.

"Oh, Adam. If it's crazy, then this must be mass hysteria because I will definitely marry you!" She resumes kissing me all over and the shock wears off enough for me to grab her by the waist and pull her even tighter against my body.

Now that she's said yes, I pull out the Asscher cut emerald ring with opal accent stones and slide it onto her ring finger. She stares at her hand for a moment before kissing me all over again. I can taste tears, but I know they're happy tears. We finish our game of "don't say a word" to celebrate our engagement; I won.

Noah (Iron Man, tonight) is the first to notice we're back from our "tour of the house" and he doesn't hide his smirk. *Busted.* It might not have been the smartest to sneak off to have sex during my parents' annual Halloween bash, but I couldn't wait another minute to ask Maya for her hand. We're both beaming, and Noah's expression turns from mischievous to curious. He catches us at the bottom of the stairs.

"Well!!! What were you two doing?" he asks in a tone that indicates he knows exactly what we were doing. Noah wiggles his eyebrows for emphasis and Maya blushes ferociously and pretends to be extremely interested in her nails. That's when he sees it: my brother, the attorney, who never misses anything, sees the ring on Maya's finger and his jaw actually drops. He takes her hand to inspect the ring more closely.

"Holy shit! Is that what I think it is?!" Maya sneaks a look at me before we both nod.

"Yeah," I say, beaming with love for Maya. "She just said yes." Maya can't stop smiling either. Noah pulls me in for a real hug, slapping my back several times.

"Baby bro! Congratulations!" He pulls Maya into our hug and she laughs warmly. "Congrats to you both! I saw a special connection the night of Damon's dinner, but I had no idea this was coming."

My mother (but tonight, Marilyn Monroe from "Gentlemen Prefer Blonde") sees us embracing at the bottom of the stairs and stops in her tracks holding a bowl of pretzels.

"Congratulations for what? What did I miss?" Maya and I look each other and this time she gives me the go ahead.

"Maya and I just got engaged, Mom," I say, and then jump back to avoid the pretzels that scatter when she drops the entire bowl.

"Oh my goodness! My youngest child is getting married! Oh my God!" Tears are in her eyes and she's practically jumping; the pretzels are being pulverized under our feet. "Where's the ring? Can I see it?"

Maya stops hugging Noah and I to show Mom her ring and Mom practically swoons. *Thanks for the kudos, Mom.*

"Oh, Adam," she says, teary-eyed. "It's so beautiful." She pulls Maya and I into a hug and I'm literally overflowing with happiness. I'm so lucky to have my family here as witnesses. We'll likely have to call Maya's parents before the evening is done. I'll probably have to *meet* her parents soon too.

For the rest of the party, Mom drags Maya and I around the house showing off Maya, her ring, and our engagement to anyone who will listen. Dad is overjoyed—I could tell he really liked Maya after she brought his favorite wine—and Henry, Jr. toasts us with champagne. We even call Damon to let him in on the news, though it's a short call since it's after midnight in Portugal.

The only person left to tell is Cory. I leave Maya in my Mom's capable hands—she'd probably slap my hand away if I tried to pull Maya away—and find Cory in the back yard. He's dressed as a pirate tonight, complete with the eyepatch and a fake parrot pinned to his shoulder.

"So...I hear congratulations are in order." I guess I shouldn't be surprised he's already heard. Despite our private proposal, we are practically the entertainment for the party at this point. He extends his hand and I shake it hesitantly. He pulls me in for a hug instead. The damn parrot's beak almost pokes me in the eye.

"I'm really happy for you, man. I know I acted fucked up last time, but seriously, Maya clearly makes you happy." I return his hug, though I still feel defensive. My brother was supposed to have my back, but instead, he insulted the woman that's now my fiancee.

"Thanks, man. She *does* make me happy." Cory leaves to grab me a beer from the cooler by the door. It's still weird between us, but he's clearly trying. I feel Maya's hand on my shoulder and turn to her.

"Hey, babe. Did you need a break from my mom? I'm sure she's got the wedding halfway planned already." Her warm laugh turns strained when Cory comes up behind me holding a beer. Instead of excusing himself, he pushes past me and speaks directly to Maya.

"Maya, Adam probably already told you, but I want to say I'm so sorry for the things I said before. Really, for how I acted that whole night. I had a bad day, a little too much wine, and I was way outta line." I doubt an apology alone will fix it, but it's a start. To my surprise, Maya smiles openly at my idiot brother.

"Thanks so much for apologizing, Cory. I don't have any brothers or sisters, but I assume it's hard to see someone coming in and messing up the family dynamic. I would never want to get between Adam and his family, especially not when you're going to be my brother some day soon." Cory seems surprised Maya accepted his apology so readily, but I know she and Dr.

Jamison have been making a lot of progress. Love and family trump heated words and stupidity every day of the week.

I kiss Maya deeply and wrap my arm around her waist before heading back inside.

"Where are we going now?" she asks. Her eyes are shining with love and trust that I know will never get old.

"Wherever you want, babe. As long as we're together."

Acknowledgements

I want to thank my amazing husband, who put up with many late nights writing and proofreading in bed, forced me to remember to eat and sleep, and handled way more than his fair share of house work when I was "in the zone". He is my true love, a great partner, a devoted father, and the foundation of my support system .

So many great people from the numerous writers' Discord servers on which I participate provided invaluable feedback, beta reads, industry knowledge, an ear to my venting, and a source of laughter. Thank you so much for showing me I'm not as weird or alone as I felt sometimes. Those communities are truly magical to me.

About the Author

The epitome of a late bloomer, Katherine managed her near constant sexual frustration as an adolescent by writing spicy romance shorts to entertain herself and her close friends. This hobby continued into college, where she began posting her shorts to a blog no one visited.

Many years later, when her mother lost her battle to cancer, Katherine inherited a Kindle fully loaded with romance novels. Katherine decided to read all the stories loaded onto the eReader to feel closer to her late mother, ultimately reigniting her passion for steamy love stories and inspiring her to write her own. Her work will always feature characters with experiences and viewpoints which are often underrepresented in mainstream romance.

Katherine holds a degree in English and an MBA. Based in Houston, TX, she's a wife and mom to a gifted young man and two cats. When she's not writing, Katherine spends her limited free time reading romance novels, watching the latest entry into the MCU, and predicting the ending to Hallmark movies.

Keep in touch with Katherine and hear about current and upcoming releases on Instagram (@KatWroteThat).